CRAVING HIS
FORBIDDEN
INNOCENT

CRAVING HIS FORBIDDEN INNOCENT

LOUISE FULLER

MILLS & BOON

First published in Great Britain 2020
by Mills & Boon, an imprint of HarperCollins*Publishers*
1 London Bridge Street, London, SE1 9GF

Large Print edition 2020

© 2020 Louise Fuller

ISBN: 978-0-263-08457-3

MIX
Paper from
responsible sources
FSC **FSC C007454**
www.fsc.org

This book is produced from independently certified FSC™ paper to ensure responsible forest management. For more information visit www.harpercollins.co.uk/green.

Printed and bound in Great Britain
by CPI Group (UK) Ltd, Croydon, CR0 4YY

To Hugo.
For learning how not to have
the last word, and always being up for
a debate about Shakespeare X

CHAPTER ONE

SHIFTING THE PHONE against his ear, Bautista Caine silently dismissed his PA with a sharp upward flick of his head and turned his attention back to his sister's voice.

Not that Alicia was saying anything new in her message. It was more or less a repeat of what she'd said at the weekend—that she was so grateful, and he was the best brother, and she loved him—but it was still good to hear.

His mouth twisted. It had been a difficult, upsetting conversation, but was there any other kind when the subject was Mimi Miller?

He felt his shoulders tense against the fabric of his suit jacket.

Mimi, with her long blonde hair, even longer legs and those silky, soft lips that had melted against his in a kiss he had never forgotten... A kiss that had stifled all common sense and conscience and shaken him to his soul—

He gritted his teeth as his body stiffened like a pointer scenting game.

She was like the proverbial bad penny and probably always would be, given that nothing he'd said to his sister seemed to change her opinion of Mimi. Only a day ago she had told him quite earnestly that Mimi lacked confidence.

Yeah, right, and he was the Easter Bunny.

Nearly two years had passed since he'd dispatched his sister to New York—ostensibly on the basis that it was a chance for her to learn first-hand about the day-to-day running of the Caine charitable foundation. He'd assumed that the geographical distance and the fact that she would be meeting new and—to his mind anyway—far more appropriate people, would finally bring an end to her incomprehensible and unfortunate friendship with Mimi.

He'd been wrong.

Gazing out of the window at the massed daffodils in the garden of his family's London residence, he narrowed his dark eyes as he mulled over his sister's upcoming marriage to Philip Hennessy.

The news had been neither surprising nor unwelcome, but Alicia's blithe announcement that she wanted Mimi to be her maid of honour had been both. He wasn't sure what had shocked him more: the fact that the two of them were still friends after so many months of separation, or the fact that his sister had chosen to keep their continuing friendship secret from him.

No, that wasn't fair.

He was sure that if he'd asked about Mimi Alicia would have told him anything he wanted to know. But of course he hadn't asked. He hadn't wanted to hear Mimi's name—much less have to face the memory of the last time he'd seen her, or his own part in what had been the narrowest of narrow escapes. It had been easier to assume that out of sight meant out of mind.

Only, despite his concerted efforts to make her so, Mimi Miller was never far from his mind. How could she be? Every time he saw his father he was reminded of the damage caused by her crooked relatives—and, worse, those few hours when he'd let his basest needs over-rule his duty to safeguard his family.

He breathed out slowly against the knot in his shoulders.

As usual, when he let himself think about

his sister's twenty-first birthday party, he felt the same see-sawing mix of anger and regret. And, as usual, he told himself that it had been a one-off, a momentary lapse of good sense, that he had been caught off-guard by her looking like that, *looking at him like that*. For up until that moment in time he'd seen Mimi simply as a child.

Afterwards he had tried to tell himself that it wasn't her fault. She hadn't chosen to be related by blood and marriage to a pair of crooks, and he hadn't blamed her for what her stepfather and uncle had done.

His lip curled. No, the blame for that lay squarely with him—for introducing Charlie Butler and Raymond Cavendish to his father, for not seeing beneath their urbane charm.

Yet he couldn't completely absolve Mimi of responsibility for her actions.

Even on the night there had been a couple of moments when he'd felt uneasy—something he'd put down to her being Alicia's friend…a friend of the family. Later, though—too late, in fact—it had become humiliatingly clear that she had played a part in her family's deception.

She had almost played *him*—so very nearly played him.

And incredibly, despite everything else that had happened, it was that betrayal—*her* betrayal—and his stupidity that still hurt the most now.

He felt the knot in his shoulders tighten.

At first he'd wanted it to be a coincidence, but her rapid, unexplained exit from the party had confirmed her guilt in his mind, and as events unfolded he'd stopped looking to exonerate her.

Later, for his father's sake and for the reputation of his family, he'd tried to deter Alicia from continuing their friendship—only, of course, his soft-hearted sister had ignored his advice.

He felt a surge of irritation. Not with Alicia. He knew she didn't live in the real world. But he did. And it was bad enough having led the wolves to his door once. Now it turned out that he'd failed again by not insisting she cut all ties with Mimi.

The tension in his shoulders was inching down his spine.

He knew exactly how it would play out if the media ever found out that his sister was BFF with the stepdaughter and niece of the men who had looted the Caine employees' pension funds. It wasn't going to be hard for them to find it out if Alicia made Mimi her maid of honour—and that was why he'd just had to tell his sister that it couldn't happen.

His jaw tensed.

Hearing her so upset had hurt. But the alternative—having Mimi centre-stage at the wedding and in the photos—was just not an option. So he'd used his father's ill-health and the potential damage to the family name to get her to change her mind, and it had worked, but he'd had to come up with something to soften the blow.

He'd done that too, only it was not ideal—far from it. For it would mean letting Mimi Miller back into his life. But he was going to see it through for his sister's sake.

Easing back in his chair, he felt his heart kick against his ribs.

This time there would be no lapses—momentary or otherwise. No loss of control nor lowering of his guard. No having to live with the knowledge that he had come close to putting his family in jeopardy for a second time.

This time it was going to be different. He would be pulling her strings, and he was going to enjoy every second of it.

Mimi Miller was running late.

Literally running.

Although, thanks to the heels she had unwisely chosen to wear, it was more a stumbling dash than a full-on sprint, and already her lungs were begging for mercy.

Oh, thank goodness.

This was the street. Slowing down to an unsteady walk, she caught sight of her reflection in a shop window and breathed out shakily.

It was her own fault she'd had to rush.

Not because she'd been dithering over what to wear. Clothes weren't really her thing and she only owned two dresses—one of which she hated because it was so tied up with love and dreams and heartache. Her other dress, a navy and white polka dot one, had looked sweet when she'd tried it on at home, but then she'd seen the state of her waist-length blonde hair and, panicking, walked straight into the nearest hair salon for a last-minute and eye-wateringly expensive blow-dry.

But it had been worth it, she thought, her skin tingling with excitement and happiness. Today was the first time she'd seen her best friend in nearly two years and she wanted to celebrate.

Stepping inside the restaurant, she glanced down at her legs, feeling suddenly self-conscious. Jeans and a T-shirt, preferably several sizes too large, was her usual outfit of choice, but Tenedor was a super-exclusive Argentinian eatery, popular with celebrities for its discreet staff and the tinted windows that made life hard for the *paparazzi*. It was definitely not the kind of venue you turned up to wearing faded denim.

Her breathing lurched. Should she even *be* here? It was a long time since she'd moved in these circles—two horrible, hopeless years since Charlie and Raymond had been sent to prison and her life had changed for ever.

But she was being stupid. Nobody was going to connect her with that haunted-looking girl outside the courtroom.

Above the diminishing drumroll of her heart she gave her name to the unsmiling *maître d'* and followed him through the restaurant, her excitement at seeing Alicia overriding her panic at being so conspicuous.

She still couldn't believe that it was two years since she'd last seen her friend. After Charlie and Raymond's arrest they had spoken on the phone—a short, unhappy conversation, with her apologising over and over for what had happened and Alicia tearfully repeating that it changed nothing between them.

Since then they had talked and texted, but after moving to New York Alicia had been busy working for her family's charitable foundation, and then she had met and fallen in love with Philip Hennessy, heir to a restaurant empire, and that had obviously taken up most of her time.

Now she and Philip were engaged, and according to the save the date card she'd received the wedding was going to be in May—less than three months away.

In other words, Alicia was effortlessly hitting all the milestones of adulthood.

Mimi's chest tightened. Whereas *she* was working as a *barista* in a coffee shop at Borough Market, her youthful ambitions to become a film director having stalled before they got started.

And as for her love-life...

It wasn't even a case of the less said the better—there was literally nothing to say. Her one bungled foray into the world of sexual relationships had left her with her virginity intact and her confidence so battered that she'd decided to put that part of her life on hold indefinitely.

She sighed. Early spring made being single seem so much harder. London's parks seemed to be full of pairs of ducks and deer all cosying up together, and it didn't help that the scent of spring flowers reminded her of Alicia's birthday party.

And Alicia's birthday party reminded her of Bautista.

Her breath caught in her throat.

Bautista Caine.

Her best friend's older brother—her first crush. The man who had broken her heart and then walked away without so much as a backward glance.

Bautista...with his curving, lazy smile and steady dark gaze.

She hadn't been alone in fantasising about

him. Practically every girl in their school, and probably some of their mothers too, had drooled over him whenever he'd turned up to collect his sister, and it only took the briefest of glances at him to understand why.

He was smart, successful, and so charming that birds didn't just fly off the trees, they dropped like overripe fruit. Not that he was interested in schoolgirls or their mums. His girlfriends were all long-limbed, pouty-lipped models. Hardly surprising, then, that he'd found it so humiliatingly easy to turn down a night with his sister's gauche friend.

Her stomach tightened—only this time not with excitement.

It had been a long time since she'd allowed herself to think about Bautista and the night they *hadn't* spent together. But ever since Alicia had announced her engagement it had been getting harder and harder to hold back the memories and ignore the fact that at some point she was going to have to see him again or forfeit her friend's wedding. Because Alicia worshipped and adored her brother, and he adored her right back.

Unfortunately his feelings for Mimi were

somewhat cooler—if complete indifference even had a temperature.

She shivered. It had been one of the few positives about Alicia's absence: not having to face the man who had kissed her and then an hour later looked straight through her as if she didn't exist.

And that had been *before* he'd found out about Charlie and Raymond's appalling abuse of trust.

She felt her stomach contract. Before that night at Fairbourne he'd treated her with measured politeness, but judging by his concerted efforts to keep Alicia on a different continent for the past two years—her friend had let slip that it had been his idea for her to move to New York—he clearly thought she was not to be trusted.

But maybe by the time they did come face to face she might actually have met someone who would compare to Bautista Caine and not be found wanting. Her heart skipped. Maybe she might be able to tell him truthfully that he wasn't all that—

'Mimi!'

It was Alicia, in a beautiful yellow dress, a

smile splitting her face, her brown eyes shining with happiness and affection, and suddenly they were hugging and laughing and both talking at once.

'Oh, it's *so* good to see you.' Alicia took a step back and gazed at her with undisguised happiness. 'I thought you might be too busy to fit me in.'

'Doing what?'

'I don't know—you might have been hanging out at some indie film festival.'

Mimi laughed. 'Well, duh, that's *next* month.'

Giggling, Alicia gave her another crushing hug. 'I've missed you so much. I know we talk on the phone and stuff, but it's not the same as having you here.'

Mimi felt her ribs tighten. 'I've missed you too.'

Alicia smiled. 'You look amazing.'

'You mean I'm wearing a dress.'

'*No*, I mean you look amazing,' Alicia said firmly. 'Doesn't she?' She turned to the tall, fair-haired man standing behind her. 'Philip, this is my best friend—the very talented, soon-to-be-discovered filmmaker, Mimi Miller.

Mimi, this is Philip. The love of my life and a perfect saint.'

Mimi squeezed her friend's hand. This was what she loved most about Alicia—the way she spoke from the heart. Anyone else would be hiding their feelings, trying to play it cool, making a joke, but Alicia had always been unashamedly open and honest.

Philip stepped forward. 'Hi, Mimi.' He kissed her lightly on both cheeks. 'Alicia talks about you so much I feel like I already know you.'

'And it didn't put you off coming to lunch?' She smiled at her friend. 'You're right—he is a saint.'

'Hardly!' Philip laughed, and then he turned towards Alicia, his eyes softening. 'Alicia's the saint. She makes the world a better place, and I'm the luckiest man alive.'

Mimi nodded. 'Yes, you are,' she said quietly.

But her pulse was beating out of time and she felt a familiar ache in her chest. Would any man ever say those words to her?

It seemed unlikely. She'd only ever really loved one man, and he had made it so dauntingly clear that his interest in her had been nothing more than a moment of indiscretion to be swiftly forgotten that she had decided there and then that she was not ready for love. Maybe she never would be if it involved making herself vulnerable to such unbearable hurt.

Her jaw tightened as she remembered how for a couple of hours she'd let herself believe that her youthful fantasy of love might become reality, only for Bautista Caine to trample her heart and her pride into dust.

Even now, nearly two years later, she could still picture his face as he had stared straight through her, despite having kissed her just an hour earlier with an intensity that had left her blinded, breathless and dazed.

She could feel herself being sucked towards the familiar vortex of unanswered questions.

Why had he kissed her?

No, why had he kissed her *like that*?

With such fierce, consuming hunger.

And why hadn't he come back?

Had she been too eager? Too clumsy?

Her heart balled like a fist.

It had hurt so much. It still did, if she let herself think about it, and what made the pain a thousand times worse was him being her best friend's older brother, for that meant she had no one to confide in.

Her stomach tightened.

She'd have liked to pretend that she hadn't said anything to Alicia purely out of love, and a desire not to put her friend in the middle, but part of her had been afraid. She knew what it was to be cast out into the darkness, and she hadn't been willing to risk losing Alicia as she had lost everything else.

And anyway, there had been too much other stuff going on—important stuff. Charlie and Raymond had been arrested and their two families had been torn apart, so she'd hardly been in a position to just call up her friend and discuss *not* sleeping with her brother.

But now was not the time to be dredging up that particularly dismal part of the past, she told herself firmly. Her best friend was here in London, and she wasn't going to let anything ruin that.

Sitting down, she glanced admiringly around the restaurant. 'This is such an amazing place.'

'Never mind that. I want you to tell me everything you've been doing,' Alicia said, laying down her menu. 'Starting with your film.'

Stalling for time, Mimi picked up her water glass. There was depressingly little to say. Like everything else she touched, it had fallen apart—all her effort and hopes turning to dust just as they always did.

It was true that she had made a film—a short, largely improvised black and white movie about a group of girls on a night out in London—and, incredibly, she had managed to find a distributor for it. Only that had been nine months ago, and she was still struggling to get it released. And, frankly, the chances of that ever happening seemed to be getting less and less likely.

She felt a twinge of tension in her shoulders.

When filming had begun, both her lead actresses had been desperate to grab some arthouse credentials, but since then they had signed on to a high school movie franchise, and now their lawyers were blocking her film's release on the grounds that their clients had only made the movie as a 'favour' to her.

It wasn't true. The real reason those actresses didn't want to see the film released was that some of their 'improvised' comments were not very PG, and they didn't want to damage their new, fresh-faced images.

It was all such a mess—and far too long and boring a story for a celebratory lunch.

She shook her head. 'Later.' Reaching over, she picked up Alicia's hand and turned it over so that the diamond engagement ring glinted beneath the lights. 'Right now I want to hear all about how you two got together.'

Watching her friend talk, Mimi found herself relaxing. There was something so innocent and hopeful about Alicia. Philip was right. She *did* make the world a better place, and she *wanted* to make the world better for everyone too.

'So, how many people are coming to the wedding?' she asked as the waiters cleared the table.

Philip frowned. 'We've tried to keep the numbers down to about two hundred.'

Mimi almost laughed. But of course—their wedding wasn't just a private exchange of vows. It was a huge event in the social calendar.

She cleared her throat. 'I'm guessing you're going to have it at Fairbourne?'

Before her life had been turned upside down she'd been a regular guest at Fairbourne, the Caines' fabled ivy-clad Georgian manor. She could still remember her first visit—how dazzled she'd been by the grandeur and beauty of the house and the almost ludicrous perfection of everything in it.

Although not nearly so dazzled as she'd been when the beautiful, dark-eyed heir to the estate had kissed her all the way to his bedroom, closing the door and pulling off his clothes first, then hers.

Her stomach clenched.

She felt her fingers twitch against the smooth white tablecloth. Bautista looked sexy as hell clothed. He had the kind of lean, muscular physique and sculpted body that allowed him to wear anything and make it look better than anyone else could. But naked—

Her mouth was suddenly dry. Naked, he was just beautiful, gorgeous…all endless, smooth golden skin and curving muscles.

An image of Bautista stretching out over her flickered before her eyes and she blinked it away as she saw Alicia shake her head, her soft brown eyes suddenly bright with tears.

'Oh, Lissy, what is it?'

Philip took Alicia's hand. 'Bob had a viral infection at Christmas and he's been a bit low since. That's why we've brought the date forward to May.'

Mimi nodded, trying to calm her beating heart. She'd met Alicia's father, financier and philanthropist Robert Caine, many times, and he'd always been a generous, gentle and welcoming host. She felt her stomach knot with guilt. Of course that had been before his already frail health had deteriorated following her stepfather and her uncle's betrayal.

'And it's why we decided to have the wedding in Argentina,' Philip added. 'It'll be autumn there, so warm but not humid.'

Alicia gave him a shaky smile, her face softening. 'And Basa has very sweetly offered to let us use his *estancia* in Patagonia for the actual ceremony, and let guests stop over at his house in Buenos Aires en route.'

Mimi's mouth curved upwards automatically, responding to the joy in her friend's voice, but for a moment she couldn't breathe or speak. Alicia's words were jangling inside her head like the notes on an out-of-tune piano, but she heard herself say quite normally, 'Oh, Lissy, that sounds wonderful.'

The waiters arrived with dessert and, glancing down at her hibiscus jelly and rum baba, Mimi suddenly felt sick. She'd known all along when she'd accepted Alicia's invitation to lunch that it was only a matter of time before Bautista's name came up in the conversation, but even so she was shocked by how much it hurt to hear it spoken out loud.

Was that how he felt when he heard *her* name? Did he wince inside?

And if so was it with shame at how he'd treated her?

Or, given Charlie and Raymond's actions, was he just relieved that he'd called time before they'd actually slept together?

She doubted that having sex with the stepdaughter of one of the men who had almost ruined his family would be high up on his list of personal goals.

'It's the most beautiful place, Mimi. There's this huge expanse of sky, and the mountains in the distance, and soft golden grass in every direction.' Alicia smiled shyly. 'Basa says it's the first step to heaven.'

Her heart stilled in her chest.

No, that had been the touch of his lips on hers, she thought, heat sweeping over her skin at the sudden sharp memory of what it felt like to be kissed by Bautista.

Her hand shaking slightly, she picked up her glass and drank some wine in a hard swallow. 'I'm so looking forward to it, Lissy,' she said, with a conviction she didn't feel. 'It's going to be the most beautiful day. But is there anything I can do? I mean, I'm sure you've got heaps of people helping...'

'Actually, there is one thing we were going to ask you...'

There was a beat of silence as Philip and Alicia glanced at one another.

'Really?' Mimi leaned forward. 'So ask me?'

'We're going to have a photographer.' Philip grimaced. 'It's not really our kind of thing, all those formal staged shots, but Bob and my parents are a little old-fashioned that way.' He hesitated. 'But what we'd really like is for you to make a film for us.'

'Something personal,' Alicia said quickly. 'You know—like you did at school, with us just talking and being ourselves.' Her mouth trembled. 'You have such a gift, Mimi. You capture a moment and hold it for ever, and I thought you might be able to do that for us.'

Mimi blinked. Her hands were shaking and

her throat felt thick. 'You'd trust me to do that?' she said slowly.

They both nodded.

Meeting her gaze, Alicia gave her a lopsided smile. 'I've trusted you with my life—or have you forgotten playing lacrosse against St Margaret's?'

Mimi grinned. 'It's seared into my brain.'

Glancing over at her friend, she suddenly felt dizzy. More than anything, she wanted to say yes. She loved Alicia, and what better way to prove that than by making her shy, modest friend the star of her own film?

But she knew Alicia too well, and without a doubt this was her way of showing her some support. She didn't need to do that—not publicly, anyway, and especially not on her wedding day. It was enough for her that Alicia had always been such a loyal, true ally.

'Oh, Lissy, I'm just an amateur, really. And this is your big day.' She was trying to gather herself together.

'Isn't that exactly what I said she'd say?' Glancing at Philip, Alicia shook her head. 'I wish I could make you believe in yourself like I believe in you.'

Mimi rolled her eyes. 'You're a good friend, and it's a lovely idea, but you're biased.'

'I knew you'd say that too.'

Alicia smiled, and something in her smile snagged a tripwire in Mimi's head.

'And you're right—I am biased. But it doesn't matter because it wasn't my idea. Or Philip's,' she added as Mimi glanced at her fiancé. 'It was Basa's.'

Mimi froze. Her heartbeat was booming in her ears so loudly she was surprised everyone in the restaurant couldn't hear it.

'I don't believe you,' she said finally. And she didn't.

The Caines might not actually live in a castle, but after her stepfather and uncle had been arrested the family had pulled up a metaphorical drawbridge. Overnight she had simply stopped being invited into their world. There had been no drama about it. They were far too well-bred to make a scene. But she had known from what Alicia *hadn't* said that Robert and Bautista thought she was bad news, and she'd never had any reason to believe they had changed their mind.

Her breath felt jagged in her throat. All she

had were those few hours at the party, when she'd mistakenly believed that Bautista felt about her as she felt about him.

'And *that's* why I asked him to join us so he could tell you himself.'

Finishing her sentence, Alicia lifted her hand and waved excitedly at someone across the restaurant.

Mimi glanced in the direction of her friend's gaze and instantly felt the fine hairs at the nape of her neck stand on end. On the other side of the room, with a lock of dark hair falling across his face, his dark suit clinging to his lean, muscular body like the ivy that grew over his family's Georgian mansion, was Bautista Caine.

Her heart seemed to stop beating.

Watching him move, she felt her body turn boneless. There was a swagger to the way he walked, a kind of innate poise and self-confidence that she had never possessed—except maybe briefly, when she was behind the camera. But even in a room like this—a room full of self-assured, beautiful people—he was by far the most beautiful, with his dark, almost black hair and eyes, and his fine features

perfectly blending his English and Argentinian heritage.

But his impact on the crowded restaurant
wasn't just down to his bone structure, or those
mesmerising sloe-dark eyes, or even that easy
honeyed smile that made you forget your own
name. He had what directors liked to refer to as
presence: a mythical, elusive, intangible qual-
ity that made looking away from him an impossibility.

To her overstrained senses it seemed to take
an age for him to reach the table. Quite a few
of the diners clearly knew him and wanted to
say hello. Her pulse skipped a beat as a famous
Hollywood actress got to her feet and kissed
him on both cheeks but Bautista seemed completely unfazed.

Of course he did: this was his world. More
importantly, it wasn't hers, and no amount
of lunching with A-listers was ever going to
change that fact.

Her understanding of that was the difference
between now and two years ago when, high on
the incredible thrill of finally being noticed by
the object of her unrequited teenage affections,

she'd let herself believe that their worlds could collide without any kind of collateral damage.

She knew better now. His abrupt change of heart had been humiliating and devastating—although of course his heart hadn't been the organ involved in that particular encounter.

And that had made her humiliation complete. For although she might have been secretly hoping for a declaration of love, what she'd offered him had been sex. Simple, no-strings, walk-away-without-so-much-as-a-backward-glance sex.

And he'd turned her down.

Her heart felt like a jagged rock scraping against her ribs.

She had gone to his room willingly, eagerly, hoping, almost believing, that she could pull it off. But of course all she'd managed to do was prove to herself that, as usual, she was punching above her weight.

'Basa.'

'Philip.'

She watched numbly as the two men embraced.

'No, don't get up, Lissy.' Leaning forward, Basa kissed his sister gently on both cheeks, and then Mimi felt her body tense as finally he turned towards her.

As their eyes met the chatter of the dining room seemed to recede.

Mimi stared at him in silence. It wasn't fair.

It wasn't fair for him to be so devastatingly good-looking. She wanted to hate him. She *needed* to hate him. Only it was hard to treat him as the despicable human being he was when he was packaged so delightfully.

But she wasn't some love-struck girl living out a fantasy, she reminded herself quickly, and there was no excuse for feeling so jittery about a man who had treated her so badly.

'Well, if it isn't little Mimi Miller,' he said softly. 'In the flesh.'

She felt her pulse pool between her thighs. His voice was the icing on the cake. Not some simpering frosted butter but a dark molten glaze—what chocolate would sound like if it could talk.

He leaned down and she breathed in the faint hint of his cologne as his lips brushed against first one cheek and then the other. Her breath stumbled in her throat as he sat down beside her, stretching his long legs out in her direction so she quickly had to tuck hers under her chair to stop their limbs colliding.

He held her gaze for a moment, and then his dark, mocking eyes dropped to her mouth. Instantly she felt her skin begin to tingle, her nipples tightening against the fabric of her dress in a way that made her want to duck under the table and hide.

Breath burning in her throat, she watched him lean back in his seat, and then, turning to face Alicia, he said calmly, 'So, what did I miss, Sis?'

She shook her head. 'Most of lunch. You were supposed to be here at one o'clock.'

He grinned unrepentantly. 'And I messaged you to say I'd be late.' Reaching across the table, he grabbed his sister's hand and squeezed it affectionately. 'Hey, I'm sorry I missed lunch, okay? But, look, I can still have dessert.'

Lowering his ridiculously long eyelashes, he gazed pointedly at Mimi's untouched rum baba.

'Here. Knock yourself out.' Smiling stiffly, she pushed her plate towards him, wishing she could throw it at his head.

'Thank you.' His fingers brushed against hers as he took the plate. 'Now, isn't this civilised?'

Their eyes met, and his cool, unblinking gaze made ice trickle down her spine, for it felt as if they were having a private and far less civilised conversation.

Oblivious to the tension, Philip leaned forward, his eyes seeking out a waiter. 'Do you want coffee with that?'

Basa looked up from his food and nodded. 'I could murder an espresso.'

Philip glanced at Mimi.

'Yes, please.' She smiled stiffly, relief washing over her skin. At least coffee meant this would soon be over and she could escape Basa's taunting gaze.

'So four espressos, then.'

'Actually, could you make that just two?' Alicia nudged her fiancé in the ribs. 'We're meeting your aunt now, remember?'

'We are?' Philip looked blank for a moment and then a flicker of understanding crossed his face and he nodded slowly. 'Oh, yes, that's right. We are…meeting my aunt.'

Basa rolled his eyes. 'Really subtle, guys.'

He tilted his face towards Mimi and gave her a long, slow smile that sucked the air from her lungs.

'My sister has probably told you that she invited me along so that I could persuade you to film her wedding, but actually that was just an excuse. She thinks we need to have a little chat, just you and me—you know, to clear the air about our families' shared history.'

Mimi blinked.

Absolutely. Not.

She practically shouted the words inside her head, and she was just opening her mouth to repeat them out loud when Basa cut across her.

'And I think she's right,' he said smoothly. 'After all, a wedding is all about moving forward. But obviously if Mimi would rather not...?'

His eyes held hers, dark, uncompromising, daring her to refuse. Beside him, Alicia was staring at her, her own eyes soft and hopeful.

'Please, Mimi. You're two of my favourite people in the world, and I know you're worried about what happened with your family and mine and that's why you don't want to film the wedding.' She bit her lip. 'Look, Philip and I are going to go now, but will you promise me that you'll stay and talk? Please? For me?'

Mimi wanted to say no, to say that there was

no point, because Basa wasn't going to listen to anything she said. But the words wouldn't form in her mouth. Not because she didn't believe them or because they weren't true—she did and they were—but because this was the first time she had found herself up against both Caine siblings and she knew she couldn't fight the two of them.

Lifting her face to meet her friend's, she forced her mouth into a smile, and beneath the blood roaring in her ears she heard herself say lightly, 'Okay, I'll stay and talk. I promise.'

CHAPTER TWO

WATCHING ALICIA AND Philip leave, Mimi felt as though she was being left in the playground by her mother on the first day of school. Unlike Basa, she thought, as he leaned back in his chair like a Roman emperor at a feast being held in his honour.

Her heart was thumping like a piston. This wasn't the reunion she'd imagined with Basa—and she'd imagined quite a few of them. The majority had involved the man calmly sitting beside her and apologising, and then begging her forgiveness.

Unfortunately, as with most of her life, the reality was a long way from her fantasy. Her attempt to matchmake for her mother had ended in disaster, her one shot at becoming a film director was languishing in a lawyer's office, and her seduction of Basa had been utterly humiliating.

Was it really so surprising that instead of

sticking to her script he was coolly drinking coffee and playing mind-games?

Her breathing faltered. She already knew what it felt like to be played by Basa, and she was in no hurry to be on the receiving end of that treatment again. Clearly the most sensible thing was for one or both of them to make a dignified and swift exit. She would just have to square it with Alicia later.

Trying to ignore the sick feeling in the pit of her stomach, she turned to face him. 'Okay, I know we said we'd stay and talk, but I think we can both agree that was only for Alicia's benefit, so please don't feel you need to stay on my account,' she said quickly. 'Really, I'm not expecting you to.'

His dark eyes glittered. 'What? Not even to pick up the bill?'

Her chin jerked up.

'I didn't come here for a free lunch, if that's what you're implying,' she snapped, and then immediately wished she hadn't, because she sounded defensive and cornered, which wasn't at all the image she wanted to project.

Although, Basa's opinion of her was so low anyway what difference would it make? He might not have said as much but his cool manner and even cooler gaze made it clear he'd made up his mind about her character back when her family had so nearly ruined his, and she doubted there was anything she could do or say to change his view. In his mind she was, and always would be, damned by association.

The waiter arrived with their coffee and she sat fuming, her mind belatedly conjuring up all the various smart put-downs she should have made to his last remark. He was just so insufferable. Sitting there and judging her as though he had the moral high ground, when his own behaviour had been utterly atrocious.

But why should she care what he thought of her anyway?

She watched him reach out and select one of the charming *petit-fours* the waiters had brought to the table with the coffee. Something in the tilt of his head seemed to tug at her memory, and her body tensed as time seemed to roll back on itself and she was in the ballroom at Fairbourne again. And standing on the other side of the dance floor, his dark, dishevelled hair accentuating the precision cut of his dinner jacket, his dark eyes fixed on her as though she was the only woman in the room, was Basa.

And that was why she cared.

In those few hours she had blossomed beneath his unblinking gaze, and then the miraculous, the unbelievable, had happened and he'd kissed her, said words she'd dreamed of hearing and—

Her fingers clenched into fists.

If she was going to indulge herself by reliving the past, the least she could do was do it properly and remember how, just when she'd started to believe he might actually mean those words, he'd got up and left her, and not come back.

The next time he'd seen her he'd looked straight through her. As if it hadn't been him who had cupped her face in his hands, his tongue tangling with hers while his thumbs caressed her aching nipples.

Trying to still the jittery feeling in her chest, she watched mutely as he raised his hands in mock surrender, his dark eyes gleaming. 'Someone's a little touchy. Or did I hit a nerve?'

He leaned forward, his dark hair falling across his face, his mouth curving in a way that made her spine shrink against her chair.

'I sincerely hope it wasn't *my* presence that dragged you away from the charms of Zone Six. I know we had that little "entanglement" at Lissy's birthday party, but if you're thinking we have some kind of unfinished business I'm going to have to disappoint you,' he said softly.

The handle of her coffee cup felt clumsy between her fingers. Her throat was tight and dry, and she was finding it hard to breathe normally.

Of all the arrogant—

Grinding her teeth, she stared at him in silence, a pulse of anger hopscotching over her skin. Did he truly think that was why she had come here? To offer herself to him? After the way he'd behaved.

It was suddenly hard to catch her breath. All the hurt and loneliness and confusion of that night rose in her throat, and when she looked down at her hands she saw they were shaking. Did he have any idea how it had felt? To lie there naked in his bed, her body quivering with longing, filled with disbelief that this beautiful, unattainable man had chosen her, only to discover that he'd changed his mind and not even bothered to tell her.

'I'm sorry to disappoint you, Basa,' she said

coldly, 'but I didn't actually know you were going to be here today. And even if I *had* known, any *entangling* with you really isn't that much of an incentive for me to "drag" myself across the road, let alone into the West End.'

He stilled, not just his body but his face, even his eyes, and she felt her heart begin to beat out of time.

'Funny... I don't remember you being so reticent two years ago. In fact, as I recall, you were pretty insistent.'

'*You* asked *me* to dance,' she snapped.

She could still remember her shock, and the sharp tingling excitement as he'd held out his hand. For to her it had felt like the moment when Prince Charming had invited Cinderella to dance at the ball.

Her heartbeat stuttered now.

Maybe if she'd been more worldly she might have seen it for what it was. Thanks to his sister's insistence that he make sure everyone had at least one turn on the dance floor, he had dutifully danced with practically all Alicia's friends by that point. But as he'd pressed her closer she'd been so cocooned in an enveloping, intoxicating happiness that nothing had existed except the muscular hardness of his body and the restless, persistent pulse between her thighs.

His dark gaze rested on her face.

'To dance, yes...' he said slowly.

Her pulse froze, and before she could stop them the images fast-forwarded.

Their 'duty' dance over, she'd thought he would thank her and leave, but somehow they had been on the terrace, the music had faded, and as she'd shivered in the cool night air he'd shrugged out of his dinner jacket and settled it over her shoulders. The silk lining had been warm from the heat of his body, and it had still been warm a moment later, when she'd stood on tiptoe and kissed him...

Her cheeks were hot and her skin suddenly felt as though it was too small for her body. She might have been a virgin—she still was—but she hadn't been completely clueless. There had been a couple of boys at parties, their clumsy lips pulling at hers like overgrown puppies with a chew toy, but nothing and no one had ever made her feel like that.

Her body had seemed to lose all its bones, to become one with his. It had felt as though she was melting into him, everything solid turning fluid, drowning all sense and reason—and, yes, she had been eager, frantic to finish what they'd started without any thought to the consequences.

But admitting that to Basa now wouldn't change his part in what had happened.

He might be blessed with mouthwatering looks and limitless wealth, but that was where his resemblance to Prince Charming ended. Even before Charlie and Raymond had been caught embezzling he'd had no plans to marry a scullery maid—or, in her case, the stepdaughter of an employee. All he'd been interested in was a short, sweet sexual encounter, and that had rapidly lost its appeal when he'd realised he'd have to go hunting for condoms to make it happen.

Of course he'd made up some other excuse to leave, but she knew he hadn't gone to get a bottle of champagne. The truth was that she just hadn't been beautiful or desirable enough to make him want to stay.

'It was a party. I'd been drinking,' she said icily. 'I just wanted to have a bit of fun,' she lied. 'That's what girls want to do at parties, Basa—they want to have fun.'

Around them the air hummed with a kind of anticipatory stillness as his eyes rested steadily on her face. To anyone watching it probably looked as if they were having some kind of intimate *tête-à-tête*, she thought, her fingers tightening around her coffee cup. Only she could feel the waves of animosity seeping across the white tablecloth.

'Mimi by name, and Me-Me by nature,' he said slowly. 'Look, I don't give a toss what you wanted or didn't want. Your life and how you live it doesn't interest me. I just don't want you dragging my sister down to the level of *your* family.' He shook his head. 'I don't know how you have the gall to show your face—'

'I'm not my family, and I would never do anything to upset Lissy.' She felt angry tears spring into her eyes.

He looked at her as if she was an imbecile. 'For obvious reasons I'm not about to take your word for that.' Shaking his head, he leaned back against his chair. 'Much as I want to, I can't stop Alicia being friends with you, but don't think for one moment that I can't see you for the manipulative little hanger-on that you are. And clearly I'm not the only one.'

She stared at his face in confusion.

'I don't know what you're talking about...'

'Of course you do,' he said quietly. 'Your little legal setback?' His eyes flickered over her face. 'My sister might be too sweet and trusting for her own good. Unfortunately for you, though, not all your friends are as naive as she is.'

Her heart bumping unevenly against her ribs, she glared at him. 'They're not my friends.'

'I'm sure they're not.' His dark eyes locked with hers. 'Not *now*. Not after you manipulated them into doing you a favour and then tried to exploit their success.'

She breathed out unsteadily. 'You don't know anything about them. Or me. And I don't have to stay here and listen to this—'

Pushing back her seat, she made to stand up, but before she could move he said quietly, 'Oh, but you do. You promised my sister we would talk. No, sorry—I forgot. That was just for Alicia's benefit, wasn't it?'

'This isn't a conversation. It's just you making vile accusations,' she snapped. 'Do you really think that's what she meant by us talking?'

His eyes rested on her face, and then, tilting

his head to one side, he sighed. 'No,' he admitted. 'I don't suppose it is.' He ran a hand slowly over his face. 'Look, Mimi, I'm here because I love my sister, and her happiness matters to me. For some unaccountable reason you being in her life makes her happy, so I'm willing...'

He hesitated, as though he couldn't quite believe what he was about to say.

'I'm willing, for her sake, to call a truce between us—but don't think for one moment that means I want to kiss and make up with you.'

Actually that wasn't true, Basa thought a half-second later. The kissing part anyway.

Picking up his wine glass, he glanced over at Mimi's taut face and wondered if she was thinking the same thing. Was she remembering that evening, that dance, that kiss? Or, like him, had her mind zeroed in on the moment in his bedroom when he'd slipped the straps of her dress over her shoulders and watched it pool at her feet...?

He shifted in his seat, wishing he could shift the memory of what had happened and what had so nearly happened at his sister's birthday party, but he'd been trying to do that for the last two years and it was still etched into his brain like an awkward tattoo from a gap year in Thailand. And it wasn't just her soft lips or the scent she wore that had burrowed into his subconscious.

Watching her that night, he'd found her beautiful and sexy. But, more than that, intriguing. As a teenager she'd been a regular visitor to the family home, and thanks to her tomboyish clothes, tied-back hair, clunky glasses and gauche manner, she'd been easily distinguished as apart from the 'glossy posse', as he'd christened the rest of his sister's friends.

Of course he'd had no time for anything but work after his father's stroke had forced him to take over the running of the family business. So he hadn't seen her properly for several years when she'd wandered into the ballroom at Alicia's party, looking as apprehensive as an antelope approaching a waterhole.

But that wasn't why he'd done a double take.

Picking up his cup, he downed the rest of his coffee. He needed that hit of raw caffeine to counteract the impact of that moment when Mimi Miller had metaphorically ambushed him and wrestled him to the ground.

She had been wearing a long, high-necked white dress that had seemed to ripple over the heart-stopping silhouette of her body, and her waist-length blonde hair had hung loose over her shoulders like a golden cape. But it hadn't been the duckling-to-swan transformation that had stopped him in his tracks, for at that point he hadn't actually worked out who she was. No, it had been something else—a kind of hesitancy that tugged at a memory hovering at the edges of his mind,

And then, as she'd turned to pluck a glass of champagne from the tray of a passing waiter, he'd felt his heart stop beating. The dress had been backless, provocative without the overt sexiness of a low-cut bodice or short hemline, and, watching her cautious progress around the room, he'd felt a strange mix of resentment and responsibility and an inexplicable need to stay close.

Too close.

Close enough to feel the heat of her skin. Close enough to let his hand slide around her waist and press against the satin-smooth skin at the base of her back. Close enough to get burnt.

His lungs suddenly felt as though they were full of wet cement.

He'd told himself that it was just a dance, and a duty dance at that, but even before the music had ended, and even though he'd known by then that she was his sister's friend, and therefore a complication he didn't need and normally wouldn't choose, he'd pulled her closer, moulding her body to his.

Lost in her scent, and the heat of her bare skin, he'd kissed her all the way to his bedroom. And there they would have finished what they'd started—only he hadn't had any condoms on him. He'd gone back down to the party, to grab a bottle of champagne to console them both, but then, walking back through the ballroom, he'd switched his phone on—the phone he could remember Mimi taking from him and switching off—and the world as he had known it had crumbled to dust.

Gazing down at the list of messages from his lawyer and his accountant, each one growing increasingly frantic, he'd felt his heart turn to stone. A brief call to his lawyer had made it clear that he needed to leave the party immediately, but discreetly, so as not to alert Alicia, and just as he'd been finishing the call he'd caught a glimpse of Mimi.

At the time he'd assumed she'd come looking for him, and he remembered how guilty he'd felt at leaving her alone for so long.

His heartbeat stalled. Now he would be willing to bet his entire fortune that she hadn't been looking for him, but he hadn't known that at the time. Trusting idiot that he'd been, he'd set off on his way to follow her.

Only it had turned out she'd made other plans.

Mission clearly accomplished, she had been sneaking out through the back door.

Watching her clutch the arm of a floppy-haired young man as she climbed into his made-you-look orange Lamborghini, he'd been devastated.

He took another mouthful of coffee and swallowed, wishing it could wash away the bitterness in his heart.

It had only been later, when the scandal had broken and he'd had time to think, that he'd realised he had been set up. All of it—her kissing him, her taking his phone—had just been an attempt to distract him, and as soon as his back had been turned it had been time for her to go. She'd even made up some lame excuse to Alicia about feeling ill.

The fact that he had been so easily duped had bruised his ego, but it had been the disconnect between the seemingly sweet child he'd once known and the woman she had become that had been most unsettling.

He would never forgive Mimi and her relatives for what they had done. Their greed and duplicity had nearly ruined his family. But it was the knowledge of how close he'd come to having unprotected sex with her, and the possible consequences of that act, that had convinced him to come to this lunch.

This time he was going to protect his family—and teach her a lesson for taking him as a fool.

'Okay, fine.'

Mimi's voice pulled him back to the present and, tipping his head back, he met her gaze.

'Okay fine, what?' he asked softly.

'I'm willing to call a truce if you are. But I don't really see any point in us dragging this conversation out any longer.'

'I disagree. We need to discuss you filming the wedding. She's serious, you know?' he added. 'About wanting you to do it.'

She raised her chin, and he felt the shock of her forget-me-not-blue eyes zigzag through his body like a jolt of electricity.

'I know she is, but whatever she said about it being your idea, I know it wasn't, so you don't need to worry. I'm not going to do it.'

She glanced away, and he felt his shoulders stiffen against the crisp white poplin of his shirt. Her desire to leave was so tangible it felt like a living, breathing thing on the table between them, and had this conversation been happening at any point up until a couple of days ago he would have been showing her the door. Hell, he would have been holding it open for her.

But that had been before he'd spoken to Alicia.

His jaw tightened. After his mother's death, and the series of strokes that had left his father's health permanently impaired, he had sworn to protect his sister and do everything in his power to make her happy. And he still felt the same way—perhaps even more so. It was, after all, partly his fault that their father was so fragile and that the business was only just now recovering its former strength.

Clearly he'd rather Mimi wasn't within a hundred miles of the wedding, but Alicia's happiness and his family's reputation were all that mattered to him. Suggesting Mimi film the wedding had been the first thing to come to mind as he had tried to stem his sister's tears and find an alternative to Mimi being maid of honour.

But now that he'd had time to think the idea of her filming the wedding was actually appealing on other levels too—for wouldn't it be safer to have her fully occupied rather than just floating around unsupervised, as she had been at his sister's twenty-first birthday party?

And who better to do the supervising than him? That way he could ensure her behaviour wouldn't bring his family's name into disrepute, *and* make her life as difficult and uncomfortable as she had made his.

'It *was* my idea,' he said softly.

She looked up at him, her blue eyes widening with scorn at what she obviously took to be a bare-faced lie.

'Of course it was. I mean you *love* having me around. That was obvious after—'

She broke off, frowning.

'After what?' he asked slowly.

Inhaling a shaky breath, she shook her head. 'So tell me, then, Basa, why exactly do you want *me* to film your sister's wedding?'

He shrugged. 'Why not?'

'What do you mean, "why not"?'

'I mean why wouldn't you do it?' he said patiently.

She stared at him suspiciously. 'You *do* realise you said that out loud?'

He smiled. 'I am aware of that, yes.'

She bit her lip and, watching her bite into the soft pink flesh, he felt his heart-rate double as his brain unhelpfully offered up an image of those same soft pink lips parting beneath his mouth.

Suddenly the need to have her commit to the project became as intense as the ache in his groin.

'She's your friend—your best friend—and I know she doesn't ask much from you because she doesn't ask much from anyone,' he said bluntly, watching a flush of colour seep over her cheekbones. 'But she has asked you to do this one thing.'

He could see by her expression that she was confused by his words, and then abruptly her face cleared.

'Oh, I get it. This is you trying to persuade me so that you can tell your sister what a good brother you are.' Her chin jutted. 'Well, if that's all you're worried about you don't need to pretend. I'll tell her you tried and I wouldn't listen.'

'I'm not pretending. I think you'd do an excellent job. You're a good filmmaker.'

'Right...'

She shook her head, and the defensive expression on her face chafed at something inside him.

'And you know that *how*, exactly?'

'Alicia showed me some of the films you used to make at school.' His eyes met hers. 'They're clearly amateur, but you really capture that teenage sense of waiting and wanting. There's not a wasted breath,' he said softly.

There was a beat of silence, and then his breathing stalled as she looked up at him with such sweet, desperate hope in her blue gaze that for a few half-seconds he forgot the past, and everything that had happened, and he was simply fighting against the insane urge to reach over and pull her closer, until her body fused with his just as it had two years ago.

Across the room, a champagne cork popped, and they both blinked at the same time.

Tuning out the heat pulsing over his skin, he regulated his breathing. 'Like I said, you're a good filmmaker, and this is your chance to be a good friend as well. So please say yes and make some happy memories for my sister.'

There was a beat of silence and then her shoulders slumped. He knew he'd won even before she began to nod her head.

'Okay, I'll do it.'

'Good.' Brushing aside the relief warming his skin, he glanced at his watch. 'I'll get your number from Alicia and then my PA can call you and talk flights—'

'Flights?' She cut across him, her eyes narrowing. 'What flights? To where?'

'Buenos Aires,' he said calmly. 'Don't worry, I'm paying. First class ticket, and obviously you'll stay at the house before we go to Patagonia.'

She began to shake her head. 'No, no, no. I'm not doing that. I'm not going to Argentina.'

'Really?' He frowned. 'So, have you got some kind of satellite camera on loan from NASA? Because London to Buenos Aires is one hell of a long shot.'

Ignoring her outraged expression, he pulled out his phone and swiped casually through his diary.

'I can't do anything for the next couple of days, but I can fly down from the States on Friday.'

Her eyes flashed. 'I don't care if you can fly to the moon and back. I'm not going to Buenos Aires on Friday. Or on any day you care to mention, in fact.'

'Oh, but you are—and I'll explain why. The wedding is in less than three months, and Alicia is flying out with my father in a few weeks to settle in. She's going to have enough on her to-do list without you wandering in at the last minute with a hundred and one questions that could have already been answered in advance. By me.'

He was impressed by the plausibility of his

words, and he could see they had taken the wind out of her sails.

'It's got nothing to do with you,' she managed finally. 'It's not your wedding and you don't know anything about film making.'

'Oh, I think it's got *everything* to do with me,' he said mockingly. 'Given that the whole event is going to be happening in my homes, and I have very specific and inflexible house rules.'

He saw her teeth clench.

'You can't expect me to make up my mind now. I'll need time to think about it.'

'I'm not selling you a car, Mimi.' He let his gaze drift over her face, enjoying the mix of frustration and fear in her blue eyes. 'Look, I'm a busy man, so I'm afraid you're going to have to work around my schedule—and that means you coming to Buenos Aires this Friday.'

'What about *my* schedule?' she snapped.

'I think Crema will probably be able to fill your shifts quite quickly, don't you?'

He'd deliberately made his voice condescending, and it was a measure of her fury that she didn't even register the fact that he knew where she worked.

She glared across the table. 'You are so un-speakably arrogant.'

'No, I'm just honest—but I guess that's a bit of an alien concept to you.' Their eyes locked, hers furious, his taunting. 'How *are* Charlie and Raymond, by the way? Still enjoying their stay at Her Majesty's pleasure?'

She stared at him, a flush of pink spreading like a sunset over her incredible cheekbones. 'You are a horrible man.'

'And *you* are bad news.' He held her gaze, ignoring the pull of her scornful pout, wishing she didn't look quite so sexy when she was angry. 'So, if we're done trading insults, let me tell you how this is going to work. The last thing my family needs on my sister's wedding day is a scandal.'

And it wasn't going to happen on *his* watch. He'd learned his lesson two years ago, when his hasty, mismanaged, ego-led decision to employ Charlie and Raymond had so spectacularly backfired. He'd been responsible for that disaster, and the collateral damage it had caused, and it was his job—his duty—to prevent anything like that happening again.

He looked up, his eyes holding hers. 'Particularly one involving *you*. So I need you to conduct yourself in a proper manner. That means following my rules, and it'll be easier to explain those rules on-site. But if you don't think you're mature enough to handle one little fully paid trip to Buenos Aires, then call Alicia.' He held out his phone. 'And break her heart.'

She stared at him mutely. 'You really are quite something. All that guff about moving forward was just for Alicia's benefit.'

'Don't push it, Mimi. I'm not going to fall out with my sister over this, but if you think that means you get a free rein in my home then you really don't know me at all.'

'Thankfully, no,' she spat. 'But if you feel that strongly about me then why don't I just stay in a hotel? Don't worry. I'll pay.'

Her skin was flawless, and the soft curl of her mouth was making him lose concentration. She was beautiful and angry and he badly wanted to kiss her.

And that was what gave him the strength to lean back in his chair.

'Sadly, that wouldn't work for me,' he said softly. 'You see, I prefer to keep my friends close but my enemies closer.'

CHAPTER THREE

LEANING FORWARD, MIMI gazed out through the limousine's tinted window, a pulse of excitement scampering over her skin as the unfamiliar streets of Buenos Aires spun past her eyes.

Bautista Caine might be the most annoying, self-satisfied and judgmental man she had ever met, but right now she couldn't help grudgingly feeling just the teensiest bit grateful to him— for had *she* been paying for this trip it would have been a far less comfortable experience.

Travelling first class, with the added bonus of being a 'friend' of the Caine family, had not only made the thirteen-hour flight pass with surprising speed, but there had been a few other surprises too—like a complimentary facial and this chauffeur-driven limo waiting for her at Ezeiza Airport!

Her mouth twisted. Once, that kind of luxury had been normal to her. Her stepfather's job at Caine's, the private bank founded by

Basa's great-grandfather, had given her family an enviable lifestyle. They'd moved to Chesham Place and she'd been sent to the same exclusive school as Alicia. There had been summer holidays in the Caribbean and skiing breaks in Aspen and Verbier.

But, really, enjoyable as it had been to have so much money, the best thing for her had been seeing her mother Nancy free of her habitual disappointment in being married to a man she didn't like and certainly didn't love.

And then, almost overnight, it had gone. Everything. The house. The holidays. Her mother's happiness. And suddenly she had gone back to being one of the have-nots.

Charlie and Raymond had both been sent to prison, and she and her mother had wound up in a small terraced house in Bexley. Not that she'd minded much by then. She'd been desperate to escape the clumps of photographers lurking outside the house, and the neighbours who had gossiped about her behind their hands.

Only Alicia, the one person who had every right to reject and resent her, had stayed loyal. And that was why she was here—whatever her brother might choose to tell himself.

Her shoulders tensed against the smooth leather, the memory of their last meeting replaying inside her head. It was galling how easily he had got his own way—and, truthfully, that was what this trip was about. However Basa might choose to dress it up, he'd been throwing his weight around. Even now, two days after it had happened, it still made her go hot and cold.

The cold was understandable. On its own, his last remark had been enough to send icy shivers down anyone's spine, but the heat...

Lip curling, she blanked out the memory of her body's involuntary and mortifying response to his and sat up straighter in her seat.

It had not been the most satisfactory encounter, although it had certainly been an improvement on their previous one. At least she hadn't ended up taking off all her clothes and making a complete fool of herself.

It was not exactly a high bar to set, though, was it? Staying clothed and not offering herself on a plate to a man who clearly despised her?

Her phone rang inside her handbag. Reaching in to find it, she frowned. It was probably her mum. She'd told her she'd call her when she landed, but she really couldn't face talking to her just now.

She felt a nibble of guilt. She had yet to tell her mother what she was doing in Argentina. Nor had she told her about Alicia's wedding— mainly because anything to do with the Caines was a no-go area. She knew from experience that hearing their name would start her mother on that downward spiral of 'if only', so when her mum had assumed she was in Argentina for work she hadn't corrected her.

Glancing out of the window again, at the faded, elegant architecture, she felt her heart contract. She hated lying to her mother, and resented having to do so, but there was no point in blaming anyone but herself for this uncomfortable arrangement. If she hadn't encouraged her mum to marry Charlie, none of this would be happening.

Pulling out her phone, she glanced down at the screen and exhaled in relief. It was Alicia. 'Hi, Lissy. I was going to call you later, to thank you for the bikini.'

It was so typical of her friend, she thought, some of her panic fading as she remembered the beautiful black and white bikini she had received in the post, together with a note telling her to relax and enjoy the sun and the pool.

'Oh, I just saw it and I thought…' Alicia hesitated. 'I can't really talk for long. I'm on the way to meet Philip's aunt—for real this time. I just wanted to make sure you're okay.'

'How could I not be okay?' Mimi said quickly. 'I've got people falling over themselves to be nice to me.'

She managed to inject a teasing note into her voice, even though right now she felt as if she was about to spend the weekend in a lion's den rather than some opulent mansion.

Basa might have insisted that she stay at the Caine family home, but his decision had nothing to do with wanting to be hospitable. He just wanted to make sure she did nothing to bring his family's name into disrepute.

It didn't matter that he'd treated her appallingly. To him she was Charlie Butler's stepdaughter and Raymond Cavendish's niece. She was, and would always be, tainted by association.

'Good.' Alicia said quickly. She sounded a little breathless, as if she was rushing somewhere. 'I'm sorry about lunch. I should have told you Basa was going to be there. It wasn't fair to drop you in at the deep end like that, so thanks for staying and thanks for making all this effort for me.'

'Yeah, travelling first class and being chauffeured around is a hard ask,' Mimi said lightly. 'But, hey, someone's gotta do it.'

'I didn't mean that. I meant...' Alicia paused. 'Look, we never really had a chance to speak after the party...you know...because...'

She hesitated again, and Mimi felt her stomach clench like a fist.

Because my stepfather and uncle had helped themselves to a bunch of pensioners' savings, she finished silently.

'Anyway, I just thought we should talk about it.'

'About what?'

For a moment Alicia didn't reply, and then she said quietly, 'I know what happened with you and Basa, Mimi. At my twenty-first.'

For a moment her mind went completely blank. She felt numb. Her heart was beating with unnatural slowness, like a clock that needed winding, and she knew that her face was constricted into an expression of horror.

'I don't know what you mean,' she said slowly. 'Nothing happened.'

'Oh, Mimi, please don't.'

The hurt in her friend's voice made her stomach squeeze into a knot of misery. She swallowed. Her mouth felt dry. She couldn't believe it. She couldn't believe that after all this time Basa had told Alicia about that night.

Imagining the spin he'd have put on the story, she started to feel sick. 'What did he say?' she croaked.

'Who? Basa? Nothing. I didn't talk to him about it. I didn't have to. I saw how the two of you were together at the restaurant.'

Mimi felt her skin squeeze her bones. She was starting to shiver with shock and panic. 'We were fine,' she said quickly.

'I'm not stupid, Mimi.'

She heard Alicia take a breath.

'I know you two had an argument, and that's why you left the party without saying goodbye. Only you didn't say anything to me because you thought it would upset me, so you said you felt ill.'

'I did feel ill.' Mimi swallowed past the ache in her throat. It wasn't a complete lie. She *had* felt sick at the mess she'd made of everything. 'And I just wanted to go home.'

'But Basa thought you should stay and he had a go at you?' Without waiting for confirmation, Alicia said quickly, 'I'm sorry. He's always been protective, but since Mummy died he just wants everything to be perfect for me.'

Mimi breathed out unsteadily. She felt almost lightheaded with relief, but also guilty that Alicia was blaming herself for something that hadn't even happened. But what purpose would telling her the truth serve except to make herself feel better in the short term?

'I'm sorry,' she said quickly. And she was— although not for concealing a fictional argument with Basa, but for letting Alicia believe a lie.

'For what?'

For probably the first time in her life her friend sounded exasperated with her.

'For feeling sick? For standing up for yourself? *I'm* the one who should be saying sorry. I know he's my brother, and I love him to bits, but you could have told me. I wouldn't have taken his side, you know.'

'It's okay to take his side,' Mimi said gently. 'He's your family.'

'And *you're* my family too. I know what your stepfather and uncle did was wrong, but it had nothing to do with you.'

Mimi's fingers tightened around the phone.

Except that it did.

Maybe not here in Buenos Aires, where nobody knew her, but back in England, she was always on edge—always expecting the past to suck her back into that dark place she'd been two years ago. It didn't matter if she was on the bus or in a café. She would look up from her magazine or her coffee and find someone looking at her curiously, and instantly she would be terrified that they were putting two and two together and coming up with a headline.

It was that fear of losing her anonymity that was the reason she hadn't really fought back against those actresses. She had been too scared that if she escalated things inevitably her name would pop up in some internet search and her scandalous past would suddenly be current news again.

'I know,' she lied.

Alicja breathed out shakily. 'And who I choose

to have in my life has nothing to do with anyone—including my brother. You're my friend, and I think Basa accepts that now.'

Like hell he does, Mimi thought, remembering Basa's parting remark about keeping his enemies close.

Injecting her voice with a note of brightness she didn't feel, she said, 'Did he say that?'

'Well, not exactly,' Alicia admitted. 'But he did say you two had had a very productive talk and that you had reached an understanding. And that's the thing about Basa: if you're on his team he'll do anything for you.'

Having arranged to call back later, for a longer chat, Mimi promised to send Alicia a photo of herself in the pool and hung up. She felt as if she'd just run a marathon, but at least one positive had come out of the conversation. Alicia believed that she and Basa had 'reached an understanding'.

As if!

The only thing he wanted was to toss her into the Thames.

She could just picture his dark eyes gleaming as he fed Alicia his carefully edited version of their conversation. Her jaw clenched.

All that rubbish about them having a 'productive talk' when he'd basically told her that he didn't like or trust her. He was a disingenuous, loathsome man.

Unfortunately for her, she was going to be staying in his house, with him, for the next forty-eight hours…

She turned her glare back to the window. Outside, clusters of extraordinarily beautiful *porteños* were making their way to work—or perhaps, given the reputation of the city's nightlife, on their way home to bed.

Glancing at the back of the chauffeur's head, she wondered what would happen if she asked him to keep driving around? She would book into some anonymous little hotel off the main strip and then maybe head out to a café and sit outside in the sun with a coffee and pastry, just watch people going about their day-to-day lives.

But there was no escaping her destiny—not least because she'd promised herself that she would see this thing through to the end. Whatever Basa said, and however he behaved, she was going to stay cool and let it wash over her—for Alicia's sake.

The air bounced out of her lungs. Who knew? Maybe if they spent some time together he might alter his harsh opinion of her and start to see the person she really was.

And there were some upsides to the situation. She hadn't been on holiday for so long, but now she was in Buenos Aires, and she was going to stay in a beautiful mansion with a swimming pool.

An image of Basa in swim-shorts, water dripping slowly off his smooth, contoured body, parachuted into her head, and instantly she felt that familiar rushing sense of vertigo, as if she was standing at the top of a skyscraper and looking down. And then her heart twitched against her ribs as finally she asked herself the question she'd been dodging since the moment she'd watched him swagger into the restaurant.

Why did she still feel this way about him?

For a start, it wasn't logical or dignified. How could she feel anything but contempt and loathing for someone who had treated her as he had? It wasn't as though it had been a mistake. He had stripped her naked and kissed her until her body had felt as though it was going to combust, and then he'd got up, got dressed and never come back.

And the worst part was that she had waited for him. She had lain there in his four-poster bed like some stupid sacrificial virgin and waited.

She could still remember how it had felt. That dizzy, disbelieving euphoria. And then, as the minutes passed—first five, then ten, then twenty—her happiness had started to ooze away like air from a punctured football. Uncertainty and panic had begun to creep in, until finally she'd been able to bear it no more and she'd found her clothes and got dressed.

Her heart began to thump. Even then she hadn't really taken his disappearance at face value. Incredibly, she'd actually been *worried* about him—she'd thought something must have happened for him not to return. But of course nothing had happened.

He'd been standing in the ballroom, talking on his phone, and then he'd turned towards her. And this was the worst part—this was the part that had finally made her understand what had happened. Not by the slightest curve of his mouth or tilt of his head had he acknowledged her. He'd looked straight through her as if she wasn't there or he didn't know who she was.

Maybe if she'd been older, or more experienced, she might have felt and behaved differently. But she'd been young and desperately in love and so unsure of herself, and her self-doubt had flared beneath his dark, blank-eyed gaze. All she'd wanted to do was crawl into a dark hole and lick her wounds.

And then she had seen Alicia there, dancing and laughing, and that was when she'd turned and walked away from the ballroom, begged a lift back to London. She'd known she couldn't face her friend, for if she had she wouldn't have been able to stop herself from telling Alicia everything. Having lost so much in her life already, she hadn't felt able to risk having that conversation and losing her best friend too.

She shivered. Sometimes she felt as if she was jinxed. What other explanation could there be for the way her world so frequently and effortlessly imploded? She was the common denominator in all of it. Her father leaving, Charlie and Raymond creating the wrong kind of headlines, and now her film, idling in some lawyer's office.

She felt the car begin to slow, and as it did so her pulse began to accelerate. For the last few minutes she'd been distracted by thoughts of Basa, so she hadn't really been paying attention to what was happening outside the window, but as she looked nervously through the glass she realised that they were driving down a wide, tree-lined boulevard. Set back from the road, some concealed by decorative walls, others by perfectly trimmed hedges, were several houses the size of hotels.

Oh, my goodness, this must be it.

Through the window she watched nervously as wrought-iron gates as tall as they were wide swung open smoothly. The car slid between them and a moment later stopped in front of one of the most beautiful houses Mimi had ever seen—and the biggest. The cream-coloured building seemed to stretch endlessly in both directions, and she had to tip back her head to see the rooftop.

She stepped out of the car, feeling horribly underdressed in her cargo pants and faded sweatshirt, just as a beautiful middle-aged woman appeared in the doorway. She had shining dark hair, and eyes the same colour and shape as

Marcona almonds, and she was clearly expecting Mimi.

'*Buenos días*, Señorita Miller. I hope you have had a pleasant trip. My name is Antonia and I'm the housekeeper here at Palacio Figueroa.'

Mimi felt her breath catch. *Great, Basa owns a palace.* No wonder his housekeeper looked like a movie star.

Inside, there was no point in pretending she was anything but dazzled. The house was gorgeously over the top, with cornices and swags everywhere, and a rich, vibrant colour scheme that perfectly complemented the opulent velvet furniture and Savonnerie rugs.

'I'm sure you want to freshen up, so let me show you to your rooms,' said Antonia, and smiled. 'I gather this is your first visit to Buenos Aires? I hope you enjoy your stay in our beautiful city.'

Mimi managed to smile back at the other woman, but inside she was thinking that it would be a lot easier to enjoy her stay if she didn't have to spend it twitching inwardly beneath Basa's dark, critical gaze.

Thank goodness he wasn't arriving until this

evening. With luck, she might even be able to plead exhaustion and turn in early, and then she wouldn't have to see him until the next morning.

Antonia stopped beside her. 'These are your rooms.'

Smiling politely, Mimi stepped through the door—and stopped. Her heart began to thump against her ribs. Mid-morning sunlight and a warm breeze were seeping through the open windows. The walls were painted ballet-slipper-pink, and there were several sofas and arm-chairs all covered in gold and pink striped silk.

'This is your sitting room. Your bedroom is through that door, and then you have a bath-room and dressing room next door. I'll let you settle in. Please treat the house as your own, and if you need anything at all, just ask.'

Clearly Antonia hadn't received the memo about Mimi being the enemy within, she thought as she tiptoed into the bedroom and gazed in delight at the vast, ornate four-poster bed.

After ten minutes of wandering from room to room, she decided that she liked the dress-ing room best. It was just so indulgent. A huge gilt-edged mirror ran the length and width of one wall, and opposite there were two beautiful chaises-longue—presumably so someone could sit and watch you get dressed.

Or undressed.

Without warning, an image of Basa lolling on that sofa, his dark gaze intent on her body as she slowly stripped in front of him, slid into her head and, gazing at her reflection, she felt her skin start to tingle.

Oh, for goodness' sake!

Her heart beating out of time, she turned away from the mirror and stalked out of the dressing room, cursing herself for being every kind of idiot and then some. This weekend was going to be challenging enough without her fantasising about a man who had made it perfectly clear that his attraction to her had been brief, and based on nothing more flattering than opportunity.

A slight breeze lifted the curtains and, crossing the room, she gazed down at a beautiful rectangular pool of perfect turquoise water. It looked so tempting, and it was exactly what she needed to cool off her overheated body and imagination.

Alicia was expecting a photo of her in her new bikini, and even Antonia had suggested she might like to go for a swim. Besides, Basa wasn't arriving until this evening so how would he even know?

Fifteen minutes later she had completed maybe a dozen or so languid lengths of the pool and was floating in the shallow end, her eyes closed against a sun that was gratifyingly brighter than the one at home. From the house, she heard a door open and the sound of footsteps—it would be Antonia, coming to find out if she wanted anything.

Not wanting to look as though she was taking any of this for granted, she forced her eyes open and swam over to the edge of the pool… and froze. Breathing out shakily, she squinted into the sunlight at a man she recognised only too well.

Except it couldn't be him, she thought, her heart doing a series of violent backflips. He wasn't supposed to be here until this evening.

But, whether he was supposed to be there or not, it *was* Basa, standing at the top of the steps leading down to the terrace, his dark eyes hidden beneath a pair of sunglasses, his dark suit incongruous among the loungers and sunlight.

For a moment he didn't move, and then to the loud and irregular accompaniment of her heartbeat, he made his way slowly down the steps to the pool.

She stared up at him mutely as he came to a halt in front of her upturned face.

'So,' he said, in a voice that stopped the breath in her throat, 'I see you've already made yourself at home. Having fun?'

Basa gazed down at Mimi, his eyes narrowing as he slipped off his sunglasses.

Walking into the house, he'd been talking on the phone to his PA and had simply mouthed a greeting to Antonia and gone straight up to his rooms. He had a headache that was threatening to split his skull in two, and he was tired after a night spent in transit and on his laptop. Still talking, he'd been in the process of loosening his tie when he'd glanced out of the window to the terrace below.

Instantly his brain had dropped into neutral and he'd begun spouting gibberish—much to the confusion of his assistant.

He'd hung up and, without pausing to consider the consequences, strode back downstairs, past his startled housekeeper and out onto the sunlit terrace.

Normally on a day like this he would have taken a dip himself, but the fact that Mimi was in the pool and therefore depriving him of that pleasure seemed to justify the anger boiling in his chest.

An anger that was doubly vexing because Mimi's near-naked presence in his pool was down to his own impulsive and unthinking behaviour.

His chest tightened. Ever since he'd walked out of that restaurant he'd been questioning his logic, his motives—hell, even his sanity—in arranging this weekend with her. But, confronted by Alicia's stubborn attachment to the woman now in his swimming pool, and by the memory of what had so nearly happened at his sister's birthday party, he'd acted with uncharacteristic rashness.

Firstly by suggesting that Mimi film the wedding and then by insisting that she come to Argentina.

Ostensibly, both were based on clear and infallible reasoning.

Mimi would be less visible behind a camera than in front of it, and by demanding that she came this weekend he was putting their relationship on a more formal footing. He wasn't her boss, exactly, but he wanted to make it clear that she was answerable to him. That way there could be no blurring of lines when it came to how they interacted with one another.

His heart began to beat faster.

But that was only a part of why he wanted her here. That night in Fairbourne his hunger for her had blinded him to what lay beneath that beautiful creamy skin. Now, though, he knew her true character, and he wanted her to know that he was in full possession of the facts and her charms no longer held any attraction for him.

He'd fully expected his first meeting with Mimi at his home to prove him correct. By rights he should be standing here feeling immensely satisfied at having summoned her across an ocean, his body stone-cold.

Unfortunately the ache in his groin suggested that hope might have been a little premature.

Gazing down at Mimi, devastating in a black and white striped bikini, he felt his breathing unravel, and wished he'd had the sense to keep his sunglasses on.

'I'm just taking a dip…'

Her blue eyes were watching him warily, and that together with the fact that her bikini-clad body was making him feel like some idiot in his suit only seemed to increase his irritation.

'Yes, you are,' he said softly.

'Antonia said it would be okay.' She frowned. 'I thought you weren't going to be here until later?'

'Oh, I see. So this is a case of while the cat's away?'

'No, it isn't.'

Her gaze narrowed, and he could tell she was trying not to lose her temper.

'It's fine,' he said. 'Like you say, you're just taking a dip.' Crouching down, he scooped up a handful of water, checking the temperature. 'Feels great. Maybe I'll join you.'

She shrank away from him like a vampire being offered garlic. 'Actually, I was just going to get out.'

He watched in silence, his stomach clenching with a combination of lust and anger, as she swam a couple of strokes and rose up out of the pool, droplets of water trickling down her neck and back. His breathing shifted. It was an all too familiar view—not from life, but from memory...the memory of that evening and that dress. Even now he could remember how it had felt. He wanted to touch her so badly that night, to run his fingers down the smooth curve of skin...

Not any more, he told himself, blocking his mind to the rush of heat tightening his muscles. Not in this lifetime.

'Here.' Catching sight of her robe, hanging from the back of one of the loungers, he picked it up and held it out to her, keeping his eyes locked on hers as she shrugged her arms into it.

'Thank you,' she muttered.

'No, thank *you*,' he said with mocking courtesy, wanting to make her feel as off-balance as she was making him. 'For coming out here at such short notice. It was very kind of you to juggle your busy schedule for me.'

Her eyebrows shot up and, lifting her chin, she said coldly, 'Let's get one thing straight, Basa. I'm not doing this for you. I'm doing this for Alicia, because she's my friend and her happiness matters to me more than anything else.'

Her mouth softened into the slightest of smiles as she spoke Alicia's name, pulling his gaze to her lips and the blood to his groin so that he suddenly felt lightheaded.

'Finally we have something in common,' he said,

Her eyes widened, her smile shifting into a scowl. 'You and I have nothing in common, Basa. I wouldn't treat a dog the way *you* treat people.'

Basa stared at her in silence, his jaw clenching. He could hardly believe that Mimi Miller— *Mimi Miller*, of all people—was saying this to him.

'And how exactly *do* I treat people? Actually, forget about me—let's just look at how *you* treat people. How you present yourself as someone to be trusted when all the time you're playing out your own agenda.'

She rolled her eyes. 'Oh, here we go again. You do realise I'm actually a completely separate person from my stepfather and uncle?'

'I do—and I wasn't talking about them. But since you've brought them up...' His mouth twisted. 'What is it they say? The apple never falls far from the tree? But even if it did, you also had Charlie as a role model. You probably learned how to grift before you could walk.'

'If you would just listen to me for five minutes I could explain—'

'You mean lie.' Shaking his head, he dragged his eyes away from the three sopping wet triangles of fabric masquerading as her swimwear. 'What did you think? That if you sashayed out of the pool in your itsy-bitsy bikini I'd be too busy drooling to listen to what came out of your mouth?'

He watched the colour spread over her cheeks. She was staring at him open-mouthed, as if she couldn't quite believe what she was hearing, and he couldn't say that he blamed her. His accusation had been harsh and gratuitous, but with her body so tantalisingly close to his, and his own body acting as if it had only recently woken from hibernation, he needed to remind himself of the kind of woman she was beneath that delectable skin.

And he was still smarting over her remark about how he treated people. How *he* treated people! She might have conveniently forgotten her behaviour, but he hadn't, even though part of him wanted to forget everything about that night.

But he could still remember every second.

Her soft, teasing laugh when she'd taken his phone and switched it off…the feverish, almost clumsy way she had kissed and caressed him, as if she was nervous about something. And, of course, the cherry on the cake: the fact that she hadn't given any thought to protection. She should have told him she wasn't on the pill and didn't have any condoms with her.

His shoulders stiffened. If he hadn't double-checked, who knew what might have happened? The media would have had a field-day. His body tensed as he imagined the gleeful, screaming headlines and, worse, his father's devastated expression as the news spread around the world that his son had impregnated the stepdaughter of the man who had almost destroyed his family.

She took a step forward, shoving her hands on her hips and unintentionally pulling the edges of her robe apart. He breathed in sharply, his anger forgotten as he caught a glimpse of her marvellous body. He gritted his teeth. It was beyond his comprehension why he should still feel like this. It had been two years. So much had happened in that time—so many good and amazing things, with good and amazing people—so why was he endlessly reliving a moment that should never have happened in the first place with a woman he didn't trust or like?

'I'm guessing you don't suffer from vertigo, do you, Basa?'

Her words caught him off-guard and he frowned. 'What has that got to do with anything?'

'Just that it must be so very high, up there on your horse, sitting in judgement over everyone, making assumptions about who they are based on nothing more than your own prejudices.' Her gaze rested scornfully on his face. 'It's a good job you gave up law. You clearly haven't mastered the basic principle of innocent until proved guilty.'

Wrong, he thought silently. He understood innocence, and there was nothing innocent about how Mimi had acted that night.

He shook his head. 'I was interested in corporate law, not criminal law, but I don't need to be a barrister to know that there are two kinds of people in this world. Those who need the judgement of a court to know whether they're guilty of a crime, and those who have a conscience. I think we both know that you fall into the former.'

She lifted her chin, her hands clenched into fists, and he knew that she was itching to thump him.

'I *do* have a conscience, and I *don't* feel guilty about anything I've done.'

'That doesn't surprise me.'

He took a step forward, almost enjoying the flare of fear and anger in her blue eyes as she backed away unsteadily. That was why he'd invited her here, wasn't it? To let her know where she stood and to demonstrate his complete and utter contempt for her.

'But let's forget about the past for the moment. I want to talk about the present, and how you're going to behave for the next few months.'

'I know how to behave.' She glared at him.

'Good. Make sure you keep it that way. Because I'm only interested in two things, sweetheart: my sister's happiness and my family's reputation. And if you do anything—anything at all—to jeopardise either of those, you will wish you had never crossed my path.'

'I wish that already,' she snapped.

They were so close he could see her flawless skin and the flecks of green and gold in the blue of her eyes. As he took another step forward he heard her breath catch, and instantly his blood was beating a path to his groin. For a split second he forgot everything—his anger, her family's crimes. All he could think about was how badly he wanted to slide his hands over the damp skin of her waist and pull her against his tense, overheated body…how desperately he wanted to kiss her.

'Tough,' he said coolly. 'I'm going to be your shadow at this wedding, Ms Miller, so get used to it.' Pushing back the cuff of his suit jacket, he glanced at his watch. 'Antonia has prepared lunch. We eat at one. Make sure you're on time.'

He let his gaze drift over her damp skin.

'And make sure you're properly dressed. Or I might accidentally confuse you with dessert.'

CHAPTER FOUR

HAVING SHOWERED AND CHANGED, Mimi made her way down to the dining room at exactly one minute past one o'clock. She would have liked to make Basa wait longer, as a sort of tit-for-tat for making her wait for him at Fairbourne, but even if he made the connection it would only make her look petty.

Lunch was somewhat strained. She was itching to tell Basa exactly what she thought of him, and only by constantly reminding herself that she was here for Alicia did she hold back her indignant words.

Obviously she got it that he hated her stepfather and her uncle. They weren't exactly top of *her* Christmas card list either. But it wasn't as if you got to choose your family, and his constant sniping was getting on her nerves. Besides, what gave him the right to have a go at her anyway? It wasn't as though *his* actions had been beyond reproach.

Picking up her glass of water, she took a sip, concentrating on the chill of the liquid and not on the heat that always accompanied her memories of that night at Fairbourne. Memories of the heat of a passion that had left her breathless, swiftly followed by a different kind of heat—the warm, sticky flush of shame at knowing that Basa would rather disinherit himself than tangle with the woman whose family had brought scandal to his doorstep.

And, judging by his comments earlier, and at that lunch with Alicia and Philip, he still felt the same way. No doubt this lunch was just another opportunity for him to lay down the law. But could he not just be civil for five minutes, given that this stupid weekend had been his idea anyway?

She felt another wave of irritation rise up inside her. It wasn't as if he was the only one who had a reason to lash out. She could just as easily be giving *him* a hard time—and about his actual behaviour, not the actions of some of his relatives.

It was so tempting to tell him some home truths, and for a few highly enjoyable moments she imagined telling Basa exactly what she thought of him—with a crushing eloquence she didn't actually possess. But for now she was just going to have to think it, not say it. Getting into some kind of slanging match with him might be gratifying in the short term, but she would end up hurting Alicia.

Her shoulders tensed. These next two days were going to be a very challenging exercise in self-restraint, but thankfully there were some positives, she thought, glancing down at her starter of smoked aubergine in a *criolla* sauce.

Picturing what she would be eating if she was at home, she almost smiled. Her lunch was usually some kind of panini, bolted down with a bottle of water. Clearly, though, people like Basa didn't have toasted cheese sandwiches for lunch.

It was just a shame *he* had to be here, casting a cloud over her with his cool, assessing gaze, but at least now that she had swapped her bikini for a denim shirt dress and ankle-high western boots she felt far less exposed.

However, compared to Basa's minimalist dark suit and perfectly knotted Windsor tie, she still felt a little underdressed. Did he dress like that out of habit? Or was it a conscious choice?

A sort of modern armour designed to intimidate and inspire respect using French cuffs and hand-sewn buttonholes instead of steel plates?

She glanced furtively over to where he was discussing wine options for the evening meal with Antonia. Not that it would matter what he wore. To add to his already overflowing list of advantages in life, he had the kind of beauty that elevated him above the ordinary.

Fortunately, she had plenty to look at other than his annoyingly handsome face. Like the rest of the house, the dining room was effervescently decorated, with walls sheathed in shimmering green silk, not one but five chandeliers, and a huge transparent acrylic table that looked as though it was made of moving water. But it was the two vast Basquiat canvases that dominated the room, their striking skulls and hieroglyphics making her forget to eat.

'Do you like Basquiat?' he asked suddenly.

She nodded, her face stiffening automatically into an expression she'd perfected during her stepfather and uncle's trial.

In the restaurant and outside in the pool, she'd been so stunned to see him that it had been hard to do anything but gape. Now, though, the fact that she was fully prepared, and fully dressed, meant that she could compose her features, for she'd learned the hard way that self-preservation required composure.

In the beginning, when Charlie and Raymond had been arrested, she'd tried to hide her face as the photographers rushed forward, shouting her and her mother's names, but she'd quickly realised that there was nowhere to hide. So she'd learned to school her features, to blank her gaze and give nothing away.

It was just a pity that she hadn't been equipped with that skill on the night of Alicia's birthday—the night when she'd stripped, both literally and metaphorically, for Basa.

Pushing the memories aside, she glanced up at the Basquiats.

'They're incredible. But I would have thought they were a little too edgy for your taste.'

His level gaze rested on her face. 'Perhaps. But art is like dining. If you always eat the same food, you never expand your palate. Besides...' he smiled slowly, his dark eyes drifting down over her dress '... I like sampling new flavours.'

Her heart jerked inside her chest. Was that

what had happened that night? Was that how he had seen her? As a 'new flavour'? She thought back to his parting remark by the pool, and the ache in her chest solidified into a hard ball of anger.

He was so entitled and arrogant. Lumping her in with every other woman in his sexual back catalogue. But she would see if he liked having the same treatment himself.

Lifting her chin, she held his gaze. 'I like sampling new things too.'

The lie made her heart race faster, but what did it matter? She'd tried telling him the truth, and it had done nothing to change his low opinion of her, so frankly he didn't deserve the truth. She watched his eyes darken, felt a pulse of satisfaction and unease bumping over her skin.

For a moment he didn't reply and then, laying his cutlery down, he said softly, 'I'm sure you do. Just make sure you don't sample any at my sister's wedding.'

Mimi stared at him in silence, trying to remember her private promise to Alicia, but as she looked up into his face something inside her snapped. Thanks to his careless treatment of her she hadn't had the confidence to so much as kiss a man, much less have sex with him, for two years, and now he was warning her off.

'It's none of your business what I do or who I do it with,' she snarled. 'You are not my keeper.'

It was the wrong answer—she knew that even before he leaned forward, his gaze narrowing as though he was tracking her with a long-range rifle.

'It is my business if you start hitting on my guests.'

Her heart was beating so hard she could feel her ribs quivering. Was he for real?

'If anyone's going to start hitting on the guests it will probably be you,' she snapped, the words spilling from her mouth like milk boiling over in a pan. 'Or have you forgotten what happened at Alicia's party?'

He stared at her in silence and she felt her pulse accelerate, the palms of her hands grow damp. It was like being in some horrible nightmare when you couldn't wake yourself up. Only she wasn't asleep, and this conversation was going nowhere—unless reliving the humiliation of that night was her goal.

But what would be the point of rehashing

the past? It was history, fixed for ever in time. What mattered was what was happening here and now—or rather, what wasn't happening. Not any more anyway.

'You know, I'd have thought a busy man like yourself wouldn't have time for playing games,' she said, leaning back in her chair, wanting more distance between herself and his unsettling dark gaze.

'I'm not playing games,' he said softly.

'Oh, but you are. Nasty, horrible, bullying games.'

He laughed, the sound echoing harshly around the beautiful room, and her heart began to thump hard inside her chest.

'How exactly am I bullying you, Mimi? Please, I'm curious. Was it your first-class flight? Did you find that too *oppressive*?' he said mockingly. 'Or does coming here to my beautiful home and being waited on by my staff make you feel *threatened*?'

She glared at him. 'I didn't want to come out to Argentina. You made me feel like I had to.'

'You did have to,' he said coolly. 'I have—'

'*Rules*. Yes, I know.' She spat the words at him dismissively. 'You told me. And I believe you. A stuffed shirt like you probably has a library of rule books—but surely none that required me to come out here in person.' Meeting his eyes, she shook her head. 'No, there's only one reason you dragged me out here, and it's got nothing to do with how I conduct myself in your Patagonian home.'

His face didn't alter, but something shifted in his eyes, and she felt her breathing lose its rhythm as she realised that her hunch was correct.

'You hate it, don't you? The fact that Alicia is my friend. And you can't bear it that you haven't been able to change her mind. That's why you want me out here—so you can spend two days trying to make me walk away from our friendship. To make me look like the bad girl. Well, it's not going to happen.'

She breathed in sharply, her pulse accelerating, as without warning he scraped back his chair against the marble floor. The force of his action nearly tipped it over and then, with swift, purposeful intent, he strode around the table until he was standing in front of her.

'It already has,' he snarled. 'You might look like an angel but you're just like the rest of your family: rotten to the core. Unfortunately, my gentle, big-hearted sister has yet to discover the *real* Mimi Miller, so I thought I'd speed up the process a little.'

Her chair rasped backwards as she stood up too, her hands curling into fists, shocked by his admission, shocked too by how desolate it made her feel to know that there was nothing she could do, much less say, to sway his mind from the view that she was just as corrupt and manipulative as her stepfather and uncle.

But it shouldn't hurt this much. After all, it wasn't as if he was the only person who believed in the no-smoke-without-fire argument. Even before the guilty verdict many of her friends and acquaintances had vowed never to speak to her again. Yet for some reason his judgement hurt more than anyone else's.

'That's the difference between you and Lissy. You. Don't. Have. A. Heart.' Lifting her hand, she punctuated each word with a jab to the taut muscles of his chest.

She gasped when he caught her hand and jerked her closer—so close she could feel the heat of his body and his anger pulsing under his skin in time with hers. Only it wasn't his anger that was scaring her. It was what lay beneath…the curling, confusing pull of desire that was quickening her pulse and making her legs shake.

Her heart jumped. He felt it too. She could see it in the sudden shrinking of his pupils. For a few quivering seconds she stared at him dazedly. They were close enough that if she tilted her head just a fraction her lips would brush against his, and she felt her body lean forward even as her mind rebelled at the thought.

She jerked her eyes up to his face as he took a step closer, his grip tightening, his beautiful curving mouth distorted into a sneer.

'My heart doesn't need to get involved when I'm dealing with a self-serving little witch like you—just my instincts. And they tell me that sooner or later you won't be able to help yourself. You'll see something you want, something bright and shiny, and you'll throw my sister under a bus to get it.'

She shook her hand free. 'That's not true. I love Alicia and I would never do anything to hurt her.'

'An admirable sentiment, I'm sure. Unfortunately,' he said slowly, 'you already have.' His eyes held hers, their dark pupils relentless and unforgiving. 'And that's the worst thing about people like you and your stepfather and your uncle. You don't understand love and loyalty, so you don't know what it feels like to have it thrown in your face.'

He was wrong. She knew exactly what that felt like—so much so that she could still feel it now, the hot ache of humiliation and a hollowness inside that sucked in every hope and dream like a black hole in space.

For a moment she couldn't speak. The pain was blocking her ability to think straight. Didn't he realise that she'd been in love with him? That her heart had been broken that night... by him?

She took a deep breath. He had recognised her hunger for it had reflected his, but he hadn't been in love so of course he hadn't seen her desperate, hopeful yearning. Her stomach tensed. She'd been a fool to come here, but she would be an even bigger fool to stay.

'And the worst thing about people like *you*,' she said, 'is that you always think you're right. Even though statistically you have to be wrong sometimes, you think you're better than every-

one else—that you're one of the good guys.'
Breathing out shakily, she shook her head.
'What a joke!'

A part of her could hardly believe what she
was saying, but she was sick of him playing
judge, jury and executioner.

'You know what, Basa? Back in England, I
thought maybe just a tiny part of you meant
what you said to Lissy about clearing the air.
That you might be willing to give me a chance
to show you who I really am. But you don't
want to do that, do you?'

'No, I don't,' he said softly, his eyes locked
on hers. 'What would be the point? You see, I
already *know* who you are.'

Actually, you don't.

The words formed inside her head, but before
she had a chance to say them out loud her eyes
snagged on the heat in his gaze. And without
pausing, much less thinking, she took a step
forward and kissed him.

Her mouth melted under his, her hands pulling him closer, carelessly crushing the fine
wool fabric of his jacket and then moving up
around his neck as naturally as if they did it
every day.

He tensed, his breath backing up in his throat, and then he gathered her closer, pressing her against him as if he was scared she would slip through his fingers. She felt her body loosen, so that there was nothing holding her together except his arm around her waist and his lips on hers.

She moaned, and as if he'd been stung he jerked away from her, his eyes widening as he gazed down into her face.

'What the—?'

Later, she would question the rawness in his voice, but in that moment she was too stunned, too devastated by the incredible stupidity of her actions, to register it—too focused on the need to escape from this house, and this man, and the tangle of suffocating emotions that had caused a thick, choking panic to fill her chest.

She took an unsteady step backwards.

'You think you know me, but you don't know me at all. So let me introduce myself. Hi, my name's Mimi Miller, and my life is miserable enough as it is without having to put up with some cold-blooded arrogant bully sitting in judgement over me for the next two days. I wish I could say it's been a pleasure meeting you, but it hasn't. So, if you'll excuse me, I'll skip dessert.'

And before he had a chance to reply, much less react, she darted past him, narrowly side-stepping a startled Antonia. She registered the housekeeper's dazed expression, heard Basa call her name, but she didn't stop. She just kept moving through the hall and up the stairs, until finally she reached the sanctuary of her bed-room.

Slumping back against his chair, Basa picked up his coffee cup and then put it down again, an expression of disgust twisting his hand-some face. After Mimi's exit he'd left the din-ing room as usual, to take his coffee in the lounge, but he didn't want coffee. He wanted to know what was happening to his perfectly ordered life.

Except that whatever loosely passed as his brain these days was struggling to form a sen-sible thought.

But how was he supposed to think straight when life had thrown a curveball like Mimi Miller at him?

He gritted his teeth. The answer to that should

be *easily.* He was a twenty-nine-year-old billionaire businessman who also happened to be the head of one of the largest charitable foundations in the world. So why, then, had he just let a woman he didn't like or trust or respect turn him inside out as effortlessly as if he was some adolescent schoolboy, barely in control of his hormones?

All he knew was that nothing was turning out as he'd planned and that today's encounter with her had left him almost as stunned as the one at Fairbourne two years ago—and that her anger and her accusations had shaken him almost as much as her kiss.

His body stiffened predictably as he remembered the urgency of her mouth on his and the melting softness of her body. That certainly hadn't been on the menu, and he still had no real idea how it had happened. One moment they were eating lunch, the next arguing. So how had they ended up clasping and kissing one another as though the world was about to end?

He sure as hell didn't know, and the only person who might be able to answer the question was upstairs, probably wishing all manner of plagues upon his head.

When Mimi had stormed off he'd had to fight an almost overwhelming urge to go after her and introduce himself to *her* properly. And by *properly* he meant with both of them naked and in her extremely large four-poster bed. Or his. Then he'd show her exactly how little he had in common with a stuffed shirt, he thought savagely.

From the moment her lips had touched his he hadn't cared about her family, or her lies, or the fact that she represented everything that was wrong with the world—the greed, the solipsism, the lack of responsibility for one's actions. All he'd cared about was tasting more of her.

Thankfully Antonia had been there, and despite the feverish hunger gripping his body he'd been conscious of his housekeeper's carefully averted gaze and had sat back down and finished his meal.

His fingers tightened against the thin porcelain handle of the coffee cup. He shouldn't care about what she'd said, and yet he could still hear Mimi's words inside his head. And each time he thought about them, and the accompanying expression on her maddeningly beautiful face, his anger seemed to grow exponentially, so that he could feel it rising like a dark wave inside him.

He wasn't a bully, or arrogant, and he certainly wasn't cold-blooded—not around *her* anyway. And why had she said that her life was miserable enough already?

He shifted in his seat. He didn't know the answer to that either, but he *did* know that it wasn't fair for her to look like that. She should look like a gargoyle, so that no one—particularly not him—would be deceived by the softness of her mouth or her wide blue eyes.

Jerking his elbow to reveal his wrist, he glanced down at his watch and frowned. He'd assumed when she ran upstairs that she needed time to cool off, and that after an hour or so of sulking she would reappear. Not crushed—that would be too much to hope—but suitably chastened.

His heartbeat slowed. Time was running out.

Alicia would undoubtedly call soon, to check how everything was going, and what was he supposed to say?

Yes, everything's going really well. She kissed

me, and I kissed her back, and then she stormed off and now she's hiding in her room.

Picturing his sister's face, her soft brown eyes wide with worry, he cursed his sister's so-called friend in both English and Spanish. He hated it that she had this power over him, but he wasn't about to lie to Alicia so...

He drained his coffee, put down the cup and stood up.

Upstairs, he stood outside Mimi's bedroom door, his jaw so tight it felt as if it might shatter. Damn her. She was going to pay for making him climb the stairs and seek her out.

He knocked and waited.

But why was he waiting? This was *his* house, he thought irritably. And, turning the handle, he opened the door and stepped through it.

The sitting room was empty and, feeling irritation swelling against the stretch of silence that greeted him, he stalked across the hand-knotted rug towards her bedroom.

'Okay, you've made your point,' he said, glancing over at the bed. 'But I think—'

He broke off mid-sentence. The bedroom was empty, and so was the bathroom and dressing room, and the lack of any clothes or luggage confirmed what the knot in his stomach had already told him.

She had gone. Left. Fled.

His pulse soared, panic blotting out any residual anger.

Where had she gone?

This was not one of her better ideas, Mimi thought, hugging her bag against her chest as she glanced wearily around the crowded side street.

But the word *idea* suggested some kind of thinking had taken place, when in reality she had spent fifteen minutes working herself up into a lather about Basa's rudeness, and her own utterly incomprehensible and humiliating decision to kiss him, and then in a rush of panic simply grabbed everything that belonged to her and sneaked out of the house.

At first, as she'd stomped down tree-lined boulevards in the warm sunshine, she had felt quite pleased with herself. It had been immensely gratifying, picturing the shocked expression on his handsome face when he discovered she was missing. Easy to picture herself staying in some little hotel, just as she had imagined on the limo ride to Basa's home.

Now, though, she was hot and tired, and for some inexplicable reason all the hotels seemed to be full.

Glancing up, she spotted another one, the sixth she had tried, and edging through a large group of men, she made her way to the front desk.

Smiling at the receptionist, she glanced down at her phone at the Spanish phrase on the screen. *'Hola! Tienen una habitación para dos noches?'*

The receptionist smiled. 'You are English, yes? I am sorry, we have no rooms available. I think you will need perhaps to go further out from the centre.'

Mimi leaned against the desk, a quiver of apprehension pulsing down her spine.

'Why is it so busy? Is something happening?'

'Yes, today is the Superclásico.' Catching sight of Mimi's baffled expression, the receptionist laughed. 'It is a football match. A very important game today.'

A football match. Of course.

Leaving the hotel foyer and gazing around,

she felt her cheeks grow warm. She was such an idiot! She'd noticed earlier that everybody seemed to be wearing identical coloured shirts, but she'd been too distracted to give it much thought. Now she realised that the streets seemed to be filling up with crowds of people wearing blue and yellow shirts, some wrapped in flags, others waving them. Even moving forward was suddenly so much harder, for there were so many people.

Where was she going to stay?

Across the square, she glimpsed a flash of red and white, and above the chanting she heard the sound of police sirens. Just like that, the crowd began to move. She didn't want to go with them but it was impossible to resist the tide of bodies. Telling herself that if she just went with the flow everything would be fine, she tried not to panic. But she could feel herself losing her balance.

And then, as she started to fall forward, someone grabbed her arm from behind and hooked her through the surging tide of fans.

Head spinning, pulse racing, she was about to turn and thank her rescuer when she found herself face to face with Basa and her words of gratitude turned to ashes in her mouth.

'What the hell do you think you're doing?' he snarled.

CHAPTER FIVE

GAZING DOWN INTO Mimi's stunned face, Basa felt his pulse surge.

For a moment his relief that he had found her and she was safe fought with anger at her reckless, impulsive behaviour, and then almost immediately his anger won and, oblivious to the security team hovering behind him, he crowded her back against a shopfront, his dark eyes locking on hers.

'Have you completely lost your mind?' He almost spat the words at her.

Breathing in, he mentally replayed the fraught minutes that had accompanied his swift, discreet search of the house and grounds after he'd found her rooms empty. His initial shock had hardened to an icy fury as he'd realised he was right. She had cut and run. Packed her bag and left, without so much as a note. But then she was good at sneaking off...

His mouth tightened.

It had taken an hour to find her. An hour of driving down street after street, his eyes feverishly hunting the crowds for a tell-tale glimpse of a blonde ponytail among the mass of mostly dark heads. It had been the longest, most stressful hour of his life, and the bar was set high.

It was pure chance that he'd spotted her, and the randomness of that fact only made him feel more agitated, for with each passing minute his imagination had grown ever more flexible— particularly when it had dawned on him that the Superclásico was happening in the city.

The match was a legendary fixture in the football season. There was a fierce rivalry between Boca Juniors and River Plate fans that frequently erupted into violence, and the sight of Mimi being swept along on a sea of blue and yellow had made panic hum in his veins.

Shouldering his way through the crowd, he had only just managed to haul her to safety. But now, instead of thanking him like any normal person, she was glaring up at him as though he had just stopped her winning gold in the Olympics.

'No, actually, I haven't. Unless you think looking for a hotel room is a sign of madness.'

She shrugged her arm free and took a step backwards, her wide blue eyes resting on his face.

He stared at her in silence, trying to swallow the adrenaline and ignore the scent of her warm, jasmine-scented skin at the same time.

Much as he would like to bury his face against her throat and forget what was happening, right now, there were more pressing matters to address. Like the fact that she would almost certainly have been trampled underfoot had he not found her when he had.

'Do you have any idea what's going on here?' He gestured past her head to where clumps of police officers were shepherding fans away from the square.

She lifted her chin. 'Yes, of course I do. It's the Superclásico.'

Stunned—maddened, in fact, by the tilt of her chin and the irritatingly condescending note in her voice—he said slowly, 'And what exactly is that?'

'It's a football match.'

'*Wrong.*'

Her eyes widened and flicked to his face, and

he felt a juvenile twitch of satisfaction at having taken the wind out of her sails.

'It's not just *a* football match, it's the derby between two of Argentina's best teams, who also happen to hate each other and are not shy about showing it. People get hurt. *You* could have got hurt.'

Saying the words out loud made him feel sick, but the impulse to pull her into his arms and hold her safe swiftly evaporated as he glanced down at her. She was staring up at him mutely, and the truculent expression on her face, coupled with the fact that a group of men across the street were staring at her with undisguised admiration, made his already fraying temper unravel further.

'More importantly,' he said tersely, '*if* you had been hurt it might have got out that you are here as my guest—and, frankly, that's not something I want to be made public.'

She went pale and, watching the colour drain from her cheeks, he felt a twinge of guilt at the brutality of his words. But he told himself that he didn't care. Mimi had been more than willing to play her part in deceiving his family, not to mention permanently depriving a bunch a pensioners of their savings, so she had no right to get upset at hearing a few home truths.

'The Vázquez family is as high-profile and respected here as the Caines are in England, and I don't need you jeopardising either one of my good names—particularly with the wedding so close.'

Her incredible blue eyes flashed with barely concealed scorn and, shaking her head, she gave him the sort of smile that could turn water into ice.

'And that's all that matters to you, isn't it, Basa? Your name. Sorry, I mean your *names*.' Her lip curled. 'And I thought philanthropists were supposed to care about the welfare of others…'

He held her gaze. 'Oh, I care—just not about rude, self-absorbed little troublemakers like you, who act first and think later.' His jaw clenched as he remembered the slippery rush of panic when he'd realised she had bolted. 'And who have no qualms about lying or stealing or sneaking off, but still expect some poor mug to roll up and rescue them from the mess they make.'

'That's not fair. I didn't ask or need to be rescued!'

She was gazing at him with a combination of loathing and disbelief, as if he'd just turned into a toad in front of her.

'And you are definitely *not* my idea of a knight in shining armour.'

Her voice was growing shriller, and he could see more of the men glancing curiously at them.

'Yeah, well, you're definitely not *my* idea of a damsel in distress.'

She might be young and female, and in need of rescuing, but she was hardly innocent. In fact, he doubted she knew the meaning of the word.

Shaking his head, he swore softly under his breath as a couple more men glanced over. What was he doing? He should be getting her off the street, not engaging with her in some kind of slanging match.

'Okay, that's it,' he said irritably. 'I am done with this stupid conversation.'

'That makes two of us,' she snapped.

He couldn't be sure if it was the petulance in her voice or the way she was holding her battered overnight bag in front of her like a shield that finally caused his temper to snap, but without consciously planning to do so he reached out and plucked the bag from her hands.

'Hey! What are you doing? Give that back.'

She made a grab for it and instantly he caught hold of her, wrapping his fingers around her wrist.

'Let's go!'

'I'm not going anywhere with you.'

She struggled against him, her long blonde hair slipping free of the ponytail at the base of her neck, but he simply tightened his grip and began propelling her past the determinedly blank faces of his security team towards the first of the two large black SUVs idling down a side street at the edge of the square.

'What are you doing?'

She was struggling to break free of his grip, and a voice inside his head was telling him that he was acting like some Stone Age throwback—only his fingers refused to let go of her arm.

'Escorting you to the car,' he said through gritted teeth. 'Before someone recognises you.'

Eyes narrowing, she tugged at his arm. 'This is not escorting...it's abducting.'

'Yes, I suppose it is.'

He stopped so abruptly that her flailing body collided with his, and desire, hot and potent, punched him in the stomach as she grabbed at his shirt to steady herself. For perhaps twenty seconds his exasperated eyes met her furious ones, and then she snatched her hand away as if she'd been stung, in a way that utterly infuriated him.

'Either way, I don't much care.' Glancing past her at the departing crowds, he gave her a small, mocking smile. 'And I'm not getting the feeling anyone else does either. So I suggest you get in the car—or, so help me, I will put you over my shoulder and carry you there myself.'

And then what?

The question slid into his head and his breath caught in his throat as he remembered her body twined around his as he'd carried her onto the bed in his room at Fairbourne. Blanking his mind to the memory of her bare thighs sliding around his hips, he tightened his grip on her wrist.

'You wouldn't dare,' she said. 'You're far

too worried about what somebody might see or say.'

'Try me,' he said softly.

He watched her eyes narrow.

'I already did.' She was shaking with anger, her cheeks flushed with red flags of defiance. 'And it wasn't worth the effort of stripping.'

Basa stared at her, shock and anger flooding through him. No, not anger. It was rage—the kind of white-hot fury that blanked out everything but the darkening bruise around his heart and the blue of her eyes.

'And yet you still did it,' he said, his fingers squeezing around her arm. 'You went up to my room, took off your clothes and got into bed with me.'

His throat tightened. There had been a honeyeyed sweetness to her eagerness. Her skin had been smooth, her mouth soft and her body even softer as she'd melted into him in a way that no other woman had.

'I guess the thought of spending your share of the pension pot helped you overcome whatever limited scruples you possess.'

Her face was so white it looked as if it was ossified.

'That's not why I went to your room.'

He heard the catch in her voice and knew he had the upper hand.

'Of course it wasn't.' His mouth curved into a sneer. 'You'll be telling me next you wanted to look at the view from my window.'

She took a quick breath. 'I went up to your room because I wanted to have sex with you.'

The bluntness of her words momentarily caught him off balance, but, recovering his composure, he shook his head. 'That's not true. You had no intention of sleeping with me; you were just there as a decoy.'

Her pupils flared with anger. 'It *is* true.'

'Then why weren't you prepared?' he snarled.

'Because I'd never slept with anyone before, that's why,' she said, and the shake in her voice made it sound as if she was close to tears.

The pavement seemed to ripple beneath his feet as her reply ricocheted around his head like a firecracker. In the square, the excited crowd were setting off flares, and he stared at her in confusion as trails of blue and yellow smoke began swirling around them. His head was spinning and he was struggling to keep his face composed. Shock—raw, unfettered shock—vied with disbelief.

Why hadn't she told him that on the night?

Was it true? Or was she just playing with him?

Her cheeks were flushed, but he didn't know if that was down to anger or chagrin at having blurted out something she would likely rather have kept hidden from him. All he knew was that this wasn't a conversation he wanted to have in the street, in front of hundreds of strangers and the averted gaze of his bodyguards.

He wanted answers. He wanted the truth. And once he had her safely inside the car, he intended to get it.

'We're not talking about this here,' he said curtly.

'Actually, I don't want to talk about it anywhere.'

Seriously? He stared down at her, a beat of exasperation pulsing over his skin.

'So you think you can just toss that grenade into the conversation and then—what? Bat your eyelashes and swan off into the sunset?'

She glared at him. 'I don't want to talk about it,' she repeated.

'In that case, you can *not* talk about it in the car.'

'I don't want to get in the car.'

Glancing from her face to her tightly closed fists, he swore softly. But, even though her stubbornness was exasperating, he found himself admiring her defiance. He was six foot four and, thanks to his head of security, Arturo, he knew how to handle himself. But Mimi was fronting up to him like a boxer.

'Tough. You don't have a choice. Because I'm sure as hell not leaving you here.'

Their eyes locked. Eventually she lowered her gaze and he felt her body go limp.

'Then let go of my arm,' she muttered.

Her sudden capitulation chafed at something inside his chest and again he had to suppress a swift, incomprehensible urge to pull her against him.

'Fine. But don't mess me around,' he warned.

Slowly he uncurled his hand and, giving him a baleful glare, she stalked towards the waiting SUV like a cat on a hot tin roof.

He breathed out through gritted teeth and

then made his way across the street, stopping to give instructions to his driver. He climbed into the car, glancing over at Mimi. As expected, she was scrunched up in the opposite corner, pointedly staring out of the window. Short of sitting on the roof, she couldn't have put any more distance between them, but that was fine with him.

He needed space to bring order to the chaos of his thoughts, and time to adjust to the revelation she had so casually tossed into the conversation.

His heartbeat accelerated. He couldn't comprehend that he might have been wrong about her. Surely she couldn't have been a virgin that night? It didn't make sense; she must be lying. But there had been a tension in her voice that had sounded real...

With an effort, he forced himself to replay that night at Fairbourne. He tried to remember whether she had been tense or apprehensive, or had acted in a way that might have suggested she hadn't had sex before. Could he have been so stunned by his own febrile reaction to her that he'd missed it? Had there been a moment, just a fraction of a second, before he'd asked her if she had protection, when he'd pushed against the slick warmth between her thighs and she'd gripped his arm tightly...? With what?

At the time it had felt like hunger, urgency. Now he wondered if it had been uncertainty and panic.

At the time she'd said nothing. In fact, she'd pulled him closer, kissing him frantically and—

It had never crossed his mind that he would have been her first lover. He'd thought he had her all figured out—that in the years when he'd been studying at university and then taking over from his father she'd done a lot of growing up. With that heart-stopping body, her mass of blonde hair and soft pout, he'd had no trouble imagining her being most men's fantasy come to life, so he'd assumed that she knew what she was doing, knew what men liked, and that was why she was being so responsive, so hungry, so uninhibited.

Only...what if it had been nervousness about losing her virginity that had made her so frantic?

His stomach felt as if it was full of stones.

For so long he'd been certain that she had cold-bloodedly lied to him, with that same soft mouth that had kissed him so sweetly. He had thought she was the kind of woman who would effortlessly seduce a family friend to give her crooked relations time to cover their tracks. A woman who would have thought nothing of having unprotected sex with him even though she must have known indisputably that any future baby would have been born into an irreversible feud between their two families.

That she had acted like that, with such determined ruthlessness, had been as shattering as it had unfathomable. But now he was finding out that he had been wrong about how sexually experienced she was. And the fact that he'd been wrong about that was making him question everything else he'd thought to be true about the woman sitting next to him.

His jaw was suddenly so tense it was difficult to release the breath he'd been holding in.

Had he been wrong?

Rather than questioning the 'facts', had it just been easier to accept them at face value?

Maybe… But if she really had been a virgin surely she would have said something?

'Mimi—'

He started to speak, but as the car began to move she cut him off.

'I have nothing to say to you.'

He shrugged. 'Then I'll do the talking.'

'But just so we're clear,' she said, and carried on speaking as if he'd not said a word, 'I am not stepping foot in that house again. So if you could just drop me at the airport...?'

He stared at her, his body tense with incredulous anger. Did she really think she could just explode a bomb into his world and then walk away without so much as a word of explanation?

'This is not a taxi service, and you will go where I take you.'

The hostile expression on her face did nothing to improve his mood.

'I'm not going anywhere with you except to a hotel or the airport,' she snapped back.

Her eyes were the same shifting capricious blue as the lake surrounding his house in Patagonia, and just looking into them made him want to strip naked and dive in. Or maybe it was the smooth skin of her bare legs, or her pink, kissable lips that were making him want to tear off both his clothes and hers?

'There's no point going to a hotel. None of them will have any rooms,' he said curtly.

'Then I'll wait at the airport.' Her soft mouth was fixed into a steely line.

'You won't need to wait.'

Rolling her eyes, she muttered something under her breath that sounded like 'entitled, arrogant jerk', and turned towards the window. But less than thirty seconds later she turned back to face him, a frown creasing her beautiful face.

'I don't understand…we just passed the sign to the airport.'

'Yes, we did,' he said evenly.

'But you said you were taking me there.'

He shook his head. 'No, you just made that assumption.'

As he had assumed she was sexually experienced?

The question popped into his head without warning and, gritting his teeth, he pushed it to the back of his mind. He would get answers, but with the aftershock from her revelation still juddering inside his head he didn't know up from down—knew only that it would be a bad idea to try and resolve this now.

'So where are we going, then?'

Her hands had curled into fists and he could hear the undercurrent of panic in her voice.

'Somewhere private.' He stared at her steadily. 'Somewhere you won't be able to embarrass my family. Somewhere a long way from civilisation, where nobody knows who you are. Somewhere you and I can have a nice long chat without any interruptions.'

'What do you mean by a long way from civilisation?'

It was testament to the level of her panic that she didn't even blink at his threat of a chat. He watched as she stared at him blankly, and then a flicker of alarm travelled across her face and she started shaking her head.

'No, Basa. I am *not* going to your house in Patagonia now.'

'Too late,' he said calmly. 'We're already on our way.'

Mimi felt as though a bucket of icy water had been upended over her head, like in one of those internet challenges. But at least with those you knew what to expect. How could she possibly have foreseen that he would pull a stunt like this?

She bit her lip. He couldn't be serious. Patagonia was hundreds of miles away, and he'd already told her he couldn't put his job on hold like she could.

Relief flooded through her veins.

Surely this was just part of his ongoing mission to show her who was the boss—or maybe he was trying to scare her, to punish her for sneaking off. But whatever it was, it couldn't have anything to do with wanting to talk about her virginity. Why would that matter to him?

Her skin felt as if it was melting.

It was awkward enough that she had admitted her inexperience to one of the most eligible bachelors in the world, but any conversation about her sex life was quickly going to reveal that she was still a virgin—and, frankly, that wasn't something she wanted to share with Basa Caine right now.

Actually, make that *not ever.*

It wasn't that she was embarrassed. All her closest friends, including Alicia, knew that she hadn't slept with anyone yet, but she would rather set fire to her own head than open her mouth and share that particular piece of information with a man who had kissed her and found her wanting.

For a moment she considered her options.

It didn't take long as there was only one.

She gritted her teeth. She didn't want to do it but she had to do something—and she was willing to do anything to derail his plan to take her to Patagonia…including apologise.

Taking a steadying breath, she gave him a small, taut smile. 'I know you're angry with me, and I'm sorry for disappearing like that. I probably shouldn't have left without telling you first—'

His gaze rested on her face. 'There's no "probably" about it, but I suppose I shouldn't be surprised. You're good at sneaking off when nobody's looking.'

Her heart began to beat a little faster. It was the second time he'd said that, and she still didn't know what he meant by it, but now was not the time to get distracted.

'Like I said, I'm sorry, okay? I just thought there wasn't much point in my staying when every time we talk we just end up arguing.'

And, of course, there had been the small but

embarrassing matter of her kissing him, and it would be even more embarrassing if he realised she was still a virgin.

His dark eyes rested on her face. 'We don't only end up arguing,' he said softly.

She blinked, and breathed out unsteadily. She was still shocked at her own behaviour—the kissing part, anyway. Obviously running away after she'd kissed him was completely understandable, but of course that didn't mean she could pretend it hadn't happened—particularly when he was sitting approximately three feet away from her.

Forcing herself to meet his gaze, she shrugged with a casualness she didn't feel. 'That was a mistake.'

'Define mistake,' he said softly, his eyes glittering.

Her breath seemed bottled in her throat. That would be because of getting in the car with him. It was too small a space, and he was too close, and when he looked at her like that it seemed even smaller.

Ignoring the prickle of heat seeping over her skin, she sucked in a breath, trying to stay calm. 'It was stupid and rash and I don't know why it happened,' she lied, keeping her eyes locked on his and away from the tempting curve of his mouth.

Earlier, in the crowded city streets, it had been easy to blank out the kiss he had so helpfully brought up, but now, with his lean, muscle-packed body sprawled only a few feet away from hers, she could feel the same insistent hunger curling through her body that had been her undoing in the dining room.

'I promise you don't need to worry about me doing anything else stupid or rash that might embarrass your family.'

'Oh, but I do worry, and that's why we can't stay in Buenos Aires.' His dark eyes locked onto hers, holding her captive. 'That and the fact that I intend to have a conversation that clearly needed to happen two years ago.'

Her chest was pressing so tightly against her lungs it was difficult to breathe.

'No, that's not—' she began, but he cut her off.

'I'm not going to let you draw me into another argument, Mimi. This is the airfield and that—' he gestured to a sleek white plane sitting on the runway '—is my jet. And now you have a choice to make. Either we use my jet, which will take approximately three hours, or we drive. That will take nearer eleven hours, so—'

She stared at him, her heart beating in her throat. 'You're joking. This is a joke, right?'

'No, it's not.' His dark gaze rested impatiently on her disbelieving expression. 'One way or another we are going to Patagonia as planned.' As she pulled out her phone, he sighed. 'There's no point trying to call anyone. You won't get a signal here, nor where we're going either.'

Glancing down at the screen, she tightened her fingers around the phone. He was right.

'I can't believe you're doing this.'

He shrugged. 'You're not going anywhere without me until this is resolved.'

Mimi felt dizzy. This couldn't be happening. It was too crazy, too preposterous to be real, and yet the expression on his face told her he meant what he said.

Her heart began to pound. Fifteen long minutes ago having a conversation with him in the car about her non-existent sex life had seemed like a form of torture, but compared to being trapped with him for who knew how long, in the middle of nowhere, it was clearly the lesser of two evils.

Her heart thumped inside her chest. She could refuse to go, or try and persuade the chauffeur to intervene on her behalf, but somehow she didn't think either course of action would get her what she wanted. Nor did she want to issue him a challenge, like she had earlier. The last thing she wanted was for Basa to make good on his threat to put her over his shoulder.

She stared out of the window. The instinct to run was nearly overwhelming, but where would she run *to*?

And yet she couldn't spend an indeterminate number of days—*and nights*—with him on an island in the middle of nowhere. Surely there was another solution?

'Look, we don't need to go to Patagonia to talk. You want to talk—then, let's talk now,' she said quickly. 'What is it that you want to know?'

'The truth,' he said softly.

She stared at him in silence. Somewhere deep inside she could feel a long-buried, festering anger roiling up inside her, after two years of being ostracised and judged and condemned without trial.

He made it sound so simple, but for the last two years there had been no single absolute truth—just a shifting kaleidoscope of other people's opinions and beliefs that had nothing to do with who she was or what had happened—and not once had he been interested or willing to listen to her version.

'Don't make me laugh! You don't want the truth. You've *never* wanted the truth. You've never once given me the benefit of the doubt. You're just like everyone else. You just want to judge me.'

Her chest pinched as she remembered all the assumptions that people had made about her and her mother. The neighbours and friends and journalists and lawyers and all those people she had never even met, who had read and repeated and believed that she was guilty on the basis of nothing more than whispers and assumptions.

But it was his judgement that hurt most of all.

'Mimi, listen—'

'No, *you* listen, Basa.'

She took a quick breath, pushing past the ache in her chest.

'If you want to force me to go all the way to Patagonia with you then *fine!*' She filled the word with all the frustration and fury that was filling her body. 'But you're wasting your time. I'm done talking to you. So I hope you're comfortable with silence, because that's all you're going to get from me.'

CHAPTER SIX

SHE KEPT HER WORD, smiling politely at the crew as they showed her to her seat, and then turning her face towards the window as soon as they were alone. It was deeply childish, she knew, to act that way, and judging by the look on Basa's face he thought so too, but she'd had enough of worrying about what he thought of her. Accommodating his stupid demands and apologising hadn't done much to change his opinion of her, so why not just be the rude, self-absorbed little troublemaker he thought she was?

Her head was aching and, overwhelmed with the tension and drama of the day, she leaned back against the leather headrest and closed her eyes.

What felt like thirty seconds later she heard the soft whine of wheels dropping into position and, opening her eyes, realised that she had fallen asleep.

She glanced out of the window and felt her heart bump against her ribs. They were getting ready to land.

Moments later the wheels hit the ground, and then she was climbing into another SUV.

It was late evening, and the sun had only recently set, so there was still a thin ribbon of gold on the horizon. But even with the headlights of the car at full beam she could see that beyond the darkness there was nothing except more darkness. And there was a threatening heaviness to the air, so that the night sky felt as though it was just inches away from swallowing her whole.

It felt as if they had reached the edge of the mapped world, and her stomach flipped over as the reality of her situation hit home.

Why had she allowed this to happen?

She couldn't be stuck out here with this beautiful, furious man, who disliked and distrusted her in equal measure—the same man she had kissed just hours earlier, without any regard for the consequences, just as she had two years ago.

Shivering against the cool chill of the memory of that night, she steadied her pounding heart. Two years ago she would have followed him barefoot and naked into the wilderness, for then she had been willing—impatient, even— to give him her body and her heart. But back then he hadn't wanted either, and nothing had changed except that now he wanted the truth.

She knew he was talking about what had happened that night at Fairbourne. But what if in exposing one truth he uncovered the real truth? That everything she touched turned to ashes?

He already knew about her stalled career; he didn't need to learn that the rest of her life, including her love life, was similarly stunted.

The car stopped, and when she climbed out she saw that they were parked by the side of a lake. A series of low-level lights illuminated a wide wooden jetty, at the end of which was moored a large motorboat.

Refusing to give in to the slippery panic sliding over her skin, she ignored Basa's outstretched arm and climbed into the boat. Soon they were moving smoothly across the water, the slow tick of the outboard engine blending with the gentle lapping of the water.

Around fifteen minutes later they reached the island. She had a fleeting impression of a curving silhouette of silvered wood and long low windows before Basa hustled her inside.

'I gave my staff the evening off, but I'm sure there will be something in the kitchen if you're hungry.'

When she didn't reply he shook his head.

'Okay, you've made your point, Mimi. Can we stop with all the silent treatment now? It's not as if refusing to speak to me is going to change anything, or make me disappear. And it's certainly not going to make our stay here particularly enjoyable.'

Their stay!

His words echoed loudly inside her head as she stared at him in disbelief, curling her toes inside her shoes to stop herself from throwing his remark back in his face—or, better still, throwing him into the lake outside.

He was making it sound as though this was some kind of mini-break, when in fact he'd forced her into coming here against her wishes. And now he had the gall to complain that she was going to ruin the enjoyment of *their stay.*

A pulse of anger beat over her skin as she met his gaze.

'So you're going to keep this up the whole time?'

He was looking down at her with barely concealed impatience, and as she glared back at him his eyes narrowed.

'Actually, you know what? Forget it. I mean, what was I thinking? How could I even consider having a civilised conversation with someone who was raised by wolves?'

Mimi gaped at him, momentarily winded by the injustice and hypocrisy of his statement.

'And abduction and coercion are just *so* civilised, I suppose,' she snapped, her vow to remain silent forgotten in a white flash of anger that blinded her to everything but the need to wipe that dismissive sneer from his handsome face.

He stared at her, a muscle ticking in his cheek. 'I am not doing this now. I'll show you to your room.'

Turning, he picked up her bag. She stared at his broad back and felt her body start to shake. Funny, that. She started talking and immediately he wanted to leave.

Her heart felt like a lump of lead inside her chest. All that stuff he'd said about wanting a conversation had really been about him pulling her strings, making her dance to his tune. He didn't care about her, or what had happened. Or about the anxiety he'd caused by dragging her out here and holding the threat of an inquisition over her head. And now he thought he could just send her to her room like some truculent child.

'That's right. Walk away, why don't you?' she snarled. 'That's what you do, isn't it, when you can't get what you want? Why don't you pretend you're looking for a bottle of champagne while you're at it?'

He swung round, his dark eyes glittering with fury. 'Keep your voice down.'

'Don't talk to me like I'm one of your staff.'

'I'm not. But then, my staff don't stand around screeching like a fishwife when everyone else is trying to sleep.'

'I'm not screeching.' She stabbed a finger in his direction. 'You're just so used to bullying people into doing what you want that you can't bear me standing up for myself! Oh, and by the way, I'm not a fishwife. In fact, I'm not anyone's wife. I'm actually very happy being single. But *if* I did get married it definitely wouldn't be to an insufferable jerk like you.'

He dropped her bag onto the smooth wooden floor, and walked purposefully towards her, his gaze fixed on her face. 'I wasn't proposing,' he said coldly. 'I'm not looking for a wife right now. And when I am ready to marry, it will be to someone who understands my world. Someone who shares my values.'

She stared at him mutely. For so long, right up until that night at Fairbourne, she'd imagined herself in love with this man. But whatever had possessed her to think that he might love her back? Even before her stepfather and uncle had knocked her life off course they had been from different worlds—his old money versus her newly acquired wealth.

And of course she knew exactly what kind of wife Basa would choose. Beautiful, smart, successful in her own right... And she would also have one of those names that mattered— the kind of name that got you the best table in the restaurant.

In other words, nothing like her. Or the version of her that he and practically every other person except Alicia believed her to be.

Her hands curled into fists. 'For the last time, I didn't know what Charlie and Raymond were doing. It was as much a shock to me and my mum as everyone else. You might not want to believe that, but that doesn't stop it being true, and the truth is what you said you wanted.'

His face looked as if it had turned to stone.

'Oh, what's the point? I need some fresh air.'

Fresh air and a much-needed reprieve from his presence.

She stormed back the way she'd come, through the front door and out onto the deck.

Basa swore with frustration, and then, without having had any thought of doing so, he was striding after her. 'Why should I believe you?'

A cool breeze accompanied the silence that followed his words and then she spun round, her eyes blazing in the darkness. 'Why wouldn't you?'

There was an ache in her voice like a bruise, but he ignored it. 'Evidence!'

'What evidence?' she snapped. She was staring at him as if he'd grown two heads. 'You mean being related to Charlie and Raymond?'

'No, I don't mean that. That would be petty— not to say unfair.'

He shook his head. Tension was swelling around them, crowding them as he had crowded her earlier in the street, and then in the car, and suddenly he was fighting to stay calm.

'None of us gets to choose our relations, Mimi, but we do get to choose how we act, and that's how other people judge us. On our actions.'

She breathed in sharply. 'Well, in that case, if you would stop slinging mud in my direction for a couple of seconds, you should take a good, long look at yourself.'

He took a step forward, his eyes fixed on her small, pale face. 'Meaning?'

'You took me to your room and stripped off my clothes and then you lost interest. Only you didn't even have the common decency to tell me to my face. You just left me lying there, like some half-eaten dessert, while you pretended to go and find a bottle of champagne.'

The ache in her voice made him flinch inwardly, and he felt a dull flush of colour spreading over the contours of his cheekbones as, inevitably, they reached the crux of the matter.

'But why were you even there? In my room? In my bed?'

He felt a stab of shame. It had been his decision to employ Charlie and Raymond, and his lack of judgement had caused untold suffering to so many people—not least his own father. And yet here he was, fixating on Mimi's motivation for turning that sweet smile his way.

'I told you why.' She stiffened. 'I wanted to have sex with you.'

His body hardened at the frankness of her words, his eyes dropping instinctively to the lush pink mouth that had spoken them.

'But you say you were a virgin.'

Her chin jerked up, her eyes widening with shock and hurt, and for one tiny insane moment he wanted to reach out and pull her into his arms.

'I don't just say it, Basa, I *was*. I st—' She broke off, stepping back unsteadily.

It was the second time she had made that claim, and once again he found himself questioning both her and himself. There had already been so many false positives that he didn't know whether to believe her. Could she really be telling the truth? Or was she just playing him again? Trying to soften his resolve?

'So why me? Why that night?'

It was the question he'd asked himself on so many occasions—a question he'd even considered asking his sister over the many months that had passed since that night. A question that seemed to matter even more now that she was claiming to have been a virgin.

'Why does it matter?' Her voice was unsteady now too. 'It was two years ago. Why do you care?'

He took a step closer, the taste of anger and frustration bitter in his mouth.

'The reason I left you lying there was because I was talking to my lawyer—the lawyer who had been calling me and leaving messages all evening about a "discrepancy" in the accounts.'

She stilled, her blue eyes suddenly like saucers. He could almost track her thoughts as she worked back through the timeline of those hours and days before news of the embezzlement broke.

His own thoughts stalled. No, that didn't make sense. She shouldn't need to work back through anything. According to his argument she would already have known that time was running out for her stepfather and her uncle, and that was why she had made a play for him.

Unless… *Unless he'd been wrong.*

Blanking his mind to that possibility, he leaned forward, the muscles in his arms swelling against the fabric of his jacket. 'Thanks to you, I never got those calls or messages—because you took my phone and switched it off. Or did you forget that little detail from the night? *"Oh, please, Basa, let's shut the whole world out."'*

Watching the colour drain from her face, he wanted to stop and rewind, erase his remark, but another part of him—the part that still stung from being played—wanted to hurt her.

'You know, I actually thought it was poetic.' He shook his head. 'It didn't occur to me that you meant it literally—that you were shutting the world out to give Charlie and Raymond time to cover their tracks.'

Mimi stared at him in silence. She looked stunned.

'That's not what I was doing,' she said shakily.

'Really?' Basa shook his head. 'So why didn't

you come and find me to say goodbye?' He felt a spasm of fury, remembering the moment when he'd seen that nameless guy with his hand resting on Mimi's back. 'Oh, sorry—I forgot. I already know the answer to that one. I saw you with him. About five foot eight, stupid floppy hair, even stupider orange car...'

His voice sounded raw, and he hated the note of jealousy that had crept in beneath the anger, but he didn't care about anything now except getting her to admit the truth and prove he'd been right about her all along.

'Do you see my problem, Mimi? You want me to believe you wanted me so much you were willing to give me your virginity—but if that's true, if you really were innocent, why did you sneak off with lover-boy?'

Her face was as white as paper now.

'I did want you.' She took a step closer, her hands trembling by her sides. 'And he wasn't my lover. I just overheard him saying he was going back to London. I wanted to go home so I asked him for a lift.'

'Right. So I'm supposed to believe that the pair of you driving off into the sunset was just a coincidence?'

'No.' She shook her head. 'It wasn't a coincidence. It was a necessity.'

'I don't understand.'

Her eyes flared, a sudden flash of blue in the darkness.

'Of course you don't. You're Bautista Caine. You have women chasing you on every continent. Nobody leaves you—nobody walks out of your life as if you don't matter. When you didn't come back I thought you'd changed your mind.' She breathed in sharply. 'That you'd been curious but I'd been a disappointment. I just wanted to get away.'

She stared past him into the darkness, and through the confused tangle of his feelings for her, the anger and the hurt, he heard the shake in her voice and knew she was an inch from tears.

'You weren't a disappointment,' he said quietly. How could she think that? 'And I wasn't just curious. I was captivated.'

He could still remember every pulsing second with punishing clarity. The slow slide of her skin against his, the urgency of her mouth. Had she no idea of how sweet she had been? How desperately he had wanted to fuse his body with hers and the weight of his disappointment when he'd had to bring it to a halt?

But how could she? If she was telling the truth then she'd had nothing to compare it to.

His breathing slowed. He could remember his own first time—how nervous he'd been, how anxious to do it right and to give pleasure as much as to receive it. What would he have thought if he'd been in her position?

He frowned. 'But why Alicia's birthday party? If that was to have been your first time, why did you choose that night?'

'When else was it going to be?'

In the still night air her voice scraped against his senses. Her eyes were deep blue on his, and she was so close now that he could see her whole body was trembling.

'I know Alicia's my friend, but I didn't mix in your circles. I knew you'd be at the party, and when you asked me to dance I thought it was our one chance to be together. That's why I took your phone and turned it off so...' She hesitated. 'So we didn't lose our chance.'

He knew it was what she would say if she was trying to manipulate him, but her words made sense in a way he didn't want or need to question.

'Why didn't you say something? Why didn't you tell me you'd never had sex?'

Her eyes slid away from his. 'You could have anyone. I thought if you knew I was a virgin it might put you off.'

His chest felt as though it was in a vice and he took a step closer, feeling again that need to take her in his arms.

'When I left you I did go and look for some champagne. I had every intention of coming back. And I would have done except—'

'It doesn't matter now,' she said quickly. 'It's all in the past.'

There was nothing between them now but a sliver of silence and the muscles tightening beneath his skin. He took another step closer.

'Is it?'

She blinked, and he knew without looking that his question had hooked her. He heard her swallow and suddenly his heart was hammering. His eyes were drawn unwaveringly to the heat in her eyes as she let out a staccato breath.

'Yes—yes, it is.'

'I don't believe you.'

The air was humming now.

Her lips parted. 'You never do.'

'Would now be a good time to start?' he asked hoarsely.

She stared at him, motionless, the darkness swelling around her. And then she was shaking her head, and before he had a chance to consider what that meant she'd drawn in a quick breath, stood up on her toes and kissed him.

His body tensed momentarily and then he pulled her against him, one hand splaying against her spine as he buried the other in her hair and kissed her back, pleasure spreading over his skin like ripples in a pond.

Her lips felt soft and she breathed jerkily into his mouth, catching his lip with her teeth as he clasped her head, tightening his hand in her hair as he tilted her face to deepen the kiss, wanting to taste her sweetness, to satisfy his hunger.

He could feel his tongue inside her mouth and she arched against him, moaning softly. He felt his groin harden, and instantly the need to touch more of her was urging him on like a jockey with a whip.

His fingers found the buttons of her dress and, popping them open, he breathed his way down over the skin of her throat and collarbone to the swell of her breasts. He lowered his face, blindly brushing it against the soft cotton of her bra, feeling his body harden as the nipples grew taut.

He wanted to hear her moan again and, pushing the fabric to one side, he sucked a nipple into his mouth, nipping and licking, his heartbeat filling his head as he felt her shiver against him.

He was harder than he'd ever been, and yet liquid too, so that he could feel himself melting into the darkness around them.

Raising his mouth, he found her lips with his, kissing her, tasting her, kissing the soft skin of her cheeks and throat, then back to her mouth, wanting, needing, to drain the sweetness from her lips.

Gently, he pushed up the hem of her dress, running his hand over her thigh, and as he flattened his palm against the damp cotton of her panties she moaned again.

'Mimi…'

He whispered her name, but even as his voice echoed in the darkness she was pushing him away.

Looking down at her, he saw a pink flush seeping over her cheeks. Her eyes were wide with a mixture of shock and hunger that he knew must be mirrored in his own dark gaze.

'I—' Her voice bled into the darkness. 'We can't.'

Gritting his teeth, he took an unsteady step backwards. He had never wanted to disagree with anyone more in his life, but despite the solid evidence pressing against his trousers he knew she was right. As tempting as it was to have sex with Mimi, out here in the darkness, at some point the sun would rise, and in the daylight they would both regret their hasty surrender to the heat and hunger of the moment.

They'd had their chance at Fairbourne but it wasn't meant to be—and that had been before they'd had all this history between them.

Besides, no amount of desire could blot out the facts: Mimi was related to the two men who had almost ruined his family's business, not to mention the lives of several thousand pensioners. An affair, however brief, would certainly alleviate the sexual tension between them—but at what cost? If it ever got out that they had slept together even once the media would pounce on the story and the Caine name would be dragged through the mud again.

'I know,' he said.

The relief in her eyes stung, but at least it took the edge off the ache in his groin.

'It's been a long and emotional day. Lines have got blurred.' He forced himself to hold her gaze. Injecting coolness into his voice, he said, 'You must be exhausted. Let me show you to your room.'

His senses were jangling, and the shift from passion to pragmatic almost blew his mind, but somehow he managed to find his way back into the house and to the bedroom door.

'It's all fairly straightforward. I'm just down there if you need me for anything.'

The expression on her face suggested that was about as likely as him finding mermaids in the lake tomorrow morning.

'Goodnight, then,' he said evenly.

Turning, he strode down the hallway before she could close the door in his face—or, worse, before he did something unutterably stupid, like capturing her mouth with his and finishing what they had started out on the deck.

CHAPTER SEVEN

WHEN MIMI WOKE, her room was in darkness, so that for a couple of moments she thought it was still night-time. Then, as her eyes began to adjust, she realised there was a thin line of daylight around the edge of the curtains. And with the daylight reality came rushing in.

Rolling onto her back, she stared up at the ceiling as her face flushed with heat.

Last night she had kissed Basa.

Twice in one day.

Skin tightening, her mind replayed the slow, pulsing hunger in his dark gaze and the bone-melting heat of his response when she kissed him. Thankfully she had come to her senses, pulling away from temptation before she'd done anything more. But she hadn't just wanted to kiss him. She had felt hollow with desire, as if everything solid inside her had dissolved and she was made of nothing but air. She had wanted him…wanted him to fill that aching emptiness.

She might be weak and reckless, but she wasn't completely stupid. She knew that even if they only slept together once, to satisfy their mutual hunger, it would be asking for trouble. There was no way she could cold-bloodedly file that particular experience away. Not when it would first involve admitting the small matter of her virginity to Basa.

Her cheeks felt suddenly hot.

She had almost told him last night, when he'd been grilling her about her motives for going to his room, but she was glad she hadn't. She didn't want him thinking she was holding out for him. She just hadn't met anyone else who made her want to take that next step. He was an impossible act to follow.

But she sure as hell wasn't about to admit that to him. He might be attracted to her, but she had known even without his not so subtle reminder about his preferred future Mrs Caine that she was not his type, and the speed with which he had showed her to her room suggested buyer's remorse at having responded to her so fervently.

Pushing back the duvet, she slid out of bed. Using the light creeping into the room, she made her way to the window and cautiously pushed the curtains aside.

She stared through the glass, not breathing.

Whatever she had been expecting, it had not been this.

The view was epic, staggering, intoxicating.

The lake looked like a vast blue mirror, and a dark fairy-tale wood hugged the edges of the water. It was difficult to make out the individual shapes of the trees that lay beyond. Further away, a lemon-coloured sun was warming a flotilla of snow-tipped peaks.

She bit into the smile that was curving her lip. It was beautiful, but she was not here to sightsee. And after last night Basa would probably be desperate to get back to civilisation, so there was no point getting too excited about the scenery.

She showered beneath what felt like a waterfall of warm water in the state-of-the-art bathroom, then pulled on a pair of trousers and a sweatshirt and tied her hair up in a loose bun before making her way to the living room.

The house was quiet and beautiful in a completely different way from the mansion in Buenos Aires. That was all drama and gilded glamour, whereas this was all about tapping into the surroundings. The decor was understated, but casually opulent with an emphasis on natural materials. It was also messier than the other house, she thought as she looked about, glancing at the rows of shelves that were curtseying gently beneath the weight of books.

How could one man live in two such diametrically opposed homes?

She was curious—more curious than she had a right to be or the good sense not to be. She tilted her head on one side to read the spines, looking for clues.

'Take one if you want,' said a cool, refined voice from somewhere behind her.

Cheeks burning, Mimi turned to find Basa watching her from the doorway. She felt her pulse quicken. He was wearing jeans and a dark jersey that hugged the muscles of his chest. The sleeves were pushed up to his elbows, revealing a tantalising stretch of smooth, golden skin. Against her will she found herself picturing the rest of his body.

Horrified by the direction of her thoughts,

she shook her head. Her eyes darted around the room, looking for some means of escape, but there was only one door and his shoulder was wedged against the frame, his body filling the opening. It was the perfect pose, both owning the room and blocking her exit, and as if he could read her mind his mouth curved up into one of those rare smiles that made her feel as if she was drowning beneath her own heartbeat.

'Really, I mean it.'

Pushing away from the doorframe, he came and stood beside her, his dark eyes flickering over her face. 'It's one of the pleasures of coming here—the chance to lose oneself in a book.' He held up the one in his hand. 'I'm reading this at the moment.'

Mimi frowned. On the cover a woman's profile was silhouetted against a pale green background; she had a bun like hers, but much neater, so she guessed that it was either a magical fantasy or a historical romance—two genres she wouldn't have thought appealed to a man like Basa.

Catching sight of her expression, he smiled crookedly. 'I think Alicia must have left it here last time she came. It's not my usual thing, but I realised I've been complacent in my habits and I thought it was about time I stopped judging a book by its cover.'

Her pulse scampered as his gaze rested on her face and she replayed his words inside her head.

'Do you like reading?'

She blinked. After so many tense, panic-inducing conversations it felt strange talking about something as ordinary as reading.

'Yes, but I'm really bad at choosing books.'

He looked up at the shelves, frowning, his gaze narrowed as if he was searching for something specific.

'Here, try this one.' He pulled a book free and handed it to her. 'It's a translation, but a good one. I think you'll enjoy it.'

'And why's that?' She glanced at the cover suspiciously.

'It's a well-written contemporary novel.' His eyes were steady and unblinking on her face. 'Oh, and it has a heroine who's been wrongly condemned by society.'

She kept on staring at the cover, his words repeating inside her head. *Wrongly condemned.* He had definitely said 'wrongly'. Her heart bumped against her ribcage. Was he trying to say something? Or was she reading more into it than was there?

Looking up, she met his gaze. 'Is that your way of saying sorry?'

He stared at her for a moment and then sighed. 'I'm not often wrong.'

She rolled her eyes. 'I guess that must be why you're so bad at apologising.'

There was a pulse of silence and then he spoke again. 'I'm sorry.'

Her chest tightened. 'For what? Being bad at saying sorry or for thinking I was part of the criminal underworld.'

'Both.' Basa's mouth twisted into something between a smile and a grimace. 'I'm sorry that I'm so bad at apologising, but mostly I'm sorry for lumping you in with your stepfather and uncle. You don't deserve that.'

His eyes were fixed on her face as if her re-action mattered to him, as if he cared what she thought of him. She felt an inexplicable light-ness fill her body.

'I was wrong.'

He took a step closer, close enough that she could see the rise and fall of his chest, and her heart squeezed tight with panic. Suddenly she wanted to throw his apology in his face, to stay good and mad with him. Because if she let herself feel tenderly towards this man she would end up getting hurt, just like two years ago. It wouldn't matter that she didn't love him— she was still too vulnerable where he was concerned. For he was both a symbol of her hopes and dreams and a reminder of her failures.

'I accept your apology.'

He stared at her for a moment. 'In that case would you like to join me for breakfast? I know Claudia, my housekeeper, is looking forward to meeting you.'

He was speaking with a kind of detached courtesy, as if she was a guest at his hotel, and she stared at him warily. It was at least something that he no longer saw her as public enemy number one, but in another way she almost preferred the intensity of his anger. Anything would be better than this careful politeness.

But it would sound utterly mad to say any of that out loud, so instead she just nodded.

Breakfast was delicious, and she ate hungrily.

Across the table, Basa drank coffee. He seemed distracted, and she guessed he was trying to work out how to tell her that they would be returning to Buenos Aires without losing face.

Thankfully the view from the dining area was as spectacular as the one from her bedroom.

It was not hard to see why Alicia was so excited to be having her wedding here, she thought, her eyes drawn to the smooth blue lake and then up to the vast blue sky. Getting married here would be like receiving nature's blessing on your life together.

'Would you like to go for a walk?'

Basa's voice brought her head around and she turned towards him, her eyes finding his. And with thoughts of Alicia's happiness uppermost in her mind, it was easy to nod and say, 'Yes, I would—very much.'

The sun was high in the clear blue sky, and there was no breeze to move the leaves of the sturdy *lenga* beech trees that grew right up to the edge of the lake.

Basa glanced over to where Mimi was staring across the lake, her blue eyes exactly the same colour as the water lapping over the stones.

It was a beautiful day, the perfect introduction to this majestic jagged land that he loved so much, even when the wind tore across the lake, sending waves crashing to the shoreline. There was something raw and real about life so close to the clouds, an unchanging, impervious essentiality that was a welcome contrast to the artifice and embellishment of the rest of the world.

And, judging by the smile tugging at the corners of Mimi's mouth, she thought so too—although he wasn't completely sure why that should make him feel quite as happy as it did.

'So what do you think?' He was careful to keep the curiosity out of his voice but his heart began to beat faster.

'I think it's the most beautiful place I've ever seen,' she said quietly. 'However did you find it?'

For a moment he considered whether to tell her the truth. But the fragile peace he had brokered this morning was still holding and he didn't want to do anything to put that in jeopardy. Then again, he was tired of all the misunderstandings between them—unnecessary and upsetting misunderstandings that had been caused by both of them being less than forth-coming with the truth.

He thought back to their conversation last night. Afterwards he had found it hard to sleep—and not just because of that kiss, although that certainly hadn't helped. For two years he'd convinced himself that he knew Mimi and that she was guilty, duplicitous, and self-serving. Now he was having to rethink his opinion of her.

And of himself.

He'd always believed that he was basically a good person: fair, rational, kind. Except he had been none of those things with her. He had been angry with himself for welcoming Charlie and Raymond into the business, and Mimi into his bed, and he'd turned that anger on her to punish her for his own ineptitude. Bullied her into coming to Argentina and Patagonia, and demanding a truth he had forced her to hide.

The least he could do now was tell her the truth.

'After the trial ended I brought my father and Alicia to Argentina to get some breathing space.' Seeing Mimi's face stiffen, he hesitated. 'It was Antonia who told me about this place.

Her great-uncle owned some land up here, and he had a little fishing shack on the island, only he was getting too old to make much use of it. So I made him an offer. A good offer,' he added. 'I might be an insufferable jerk, but I'm not a greedy one, and I wouldn't exploit an old man's ill health.'

Her eyes darted to his face, and he winced inwardly. He had wanted Mimi to know that he hadn't taken advantage of the old man. She already thought he was manipulative and bullying and he hadn't wanted to say anything that reinforced that view of him. But, spoken out loud, his words had sounded less like an explanation and more like another accusation.

He frowned. 'That wasn't a dig at you.'

'I know.' She gave him a small, tight smile. 'You don't pull your punches, Basa. If you wanted to bad-mouth Charlie and Raymond you wouldn't be coy about it.'

She was right. He thought back to how he had spoken to her before. He had been so harsh, so unforgiving, both in his manner and in his choice of words.

'I was angry. I still am angry with them. They had no reason to steal.' A hardness crept into his voice, and his hands were suddenly clenching so tightly that his knuckles felt as though they were about to split apart. 'They had so much more than so many other people—so much more than those pensioners.'

She hesitated, and then she reached out and grasped his fists, gently uncurled his fingers. 'I know.'

Her soft expression pulled at some thread inside him and he glanced away. 'They hurt my father, Mimi. He's never been strong, and he was shocked and devastated by what they did. He had another stroke—a bad one. I had to take over the business, the foundation...'

Charlie and Raymond had stolen more from him than money. He'd lost the freedom and independence that most twenty-somethings enjoyed and, more importantly he'd lost his father.

There was a moment of silence and then she said quietly, 'I'm so sorry, Basa.'

Her eyes were clouded with sadness and he could hear the ache of regret in her voice.

'It's not your fault, truly, but it was a difficult time.' He glanced past her at the ridge of mountains in the distance. 'That's why I bought this place. To have somewhere away from the world. Somewhere tranquil and safe.'

He hesitated. As a general rule he didn't talk about himself, and he had never told anyone that before. He'd told his father and Alicia that he'd bought the land as an investment—he hadn't wanted them to think that he couldn't cope, or that he was scared, though in fact both had been true.

'It must have been hard for you,' she said gently. 'Being thrown in the deep end like that.'

They were walking now, and he stared at her profile in silence, caught off balance by the note of concern in her voice. He knew his family loved him, but nobody ever really asked him about his feelings, and he'd always been glad, even proud about that, for it meant he was doing his job properly. Now, though, with Mimi's blue gaze searching his face, he realised that he wanted to share those buried emotions with her.

'It *was* hard. It was all such a mess. For months I wasn't sure if I could save the business. I even thought we might lose Fairbourne.'

He could still remember the cold grip of panic, the need to confide in someone and yet the pressure to stay silent. He'd been so scared, and he'd felt so alone—just like after his mother died.

'It helped that it wasn't the first time I'd had to take over. After the accident I was acting CEO for a while—just until my dad got back on his feet.'

He felt her fingers tighten around his.

'I didn't know.'

'It was a long time ago.' The worry in her eyes and the fact that she cared was messing with his head. 'Anyway, everything was fine in the end. I managed to sort it.'

'You didn't just sort it,' she protested. 'You saved it.'

'It was my responsibility.' His mouth twisted. 'It was my fault it happened. I hired Charlie and Raymond. I trusted them.'

'Why wouldn't you?'

'I should have known.'

He felt his shoulders tense, the shame and shock of his stupidity as fresh now as it had been when he'd met his CFO the morning after Alicia's party.

'There were signs, little things, but I was so desperate to prove myself, to show my father he could trust me that I just ignored them.' His eyes rested on her small pale face. 'After it all fell apart I was so focused on turning everything around I didn't realise how much it affected the way I interacted with people, but trust is hard to recover once it's lost.'

'Yes, it is,' she said quietly.

Mimi looked away. It hurt too much to see the pain in his eyes—pain caused by *her* family, by her stupid, selfish stepfather and equally stupid, selfish uncle.

She stared across the water to where small waves splashed against a series of sharp black rocks. Against the placid surface of the lake, it was easy to focus on their jagged threat— just as she had chosen to focus on Basa's outward hostility rather than the trauma that had created it. He'd lost his mother when he was not much younger than she was now, and for a time he had been responsible for looking after his family.

Remembering Alicia's remarks in the car, she felt her heart beat a little faster. He still was.

She could see now that it hadn't ever really been about him. It had been about herself, and the private fear that once again she had jinxed something that might have been perfect.

Basa seemed so strong, so determined, and she'd judged him as he had her: on outward appearances. Hearing him talk about his family's name, she had thought he was a snob; when he'd spoken about having rules, she'd thought he wanted to be in control without understanding why he needed to be. She hadn't understood his deep-seated sense of responsibility for the scandal that had so nearly ruined his father and Alicia.

She knew what it must have taken to turn his business around and restore his family name, and there could be no doubting his love for his family or his sense of responsibility for them and for the pensioners who had been robbed. He had stepped up, and it was incredible what he'd done, given how young he was.

But all injuries left scars: some visible, others less so. And she understood why he found it hard to trust people—her in particular.

All her life she had struggled to trust herself, to trust other people. Her father had started that particular ball rolling. He'd left shortly after her tenth birthday and, devastated by his rejection, her mother had turned for support to her charming but irresponsible brother Raymond, who had introduced her to his best friend Charlie.

Had she ever liked Charlie? Not really—but she'd been desperate to see her mother happy again, so she'd encouraged the relationship.

'We trusted them too. My mum and me. *I* trusted them,' she said slowly.

'You were a child.'

'At first, yes. But later I think I knew they weren't be trusted. Raymond was lovely, but he was always a chancer, and Charlie was so clever at making you believe what he said.'

His face tensed and she braced herself, expecting him to pull away, but instead his fingers locked more tightly around hers. 'But you didn't know.'

Yesterday he would have phrased it as a question, but today it was a statement, and she squirreled that away, scared by how happy it made her feel.

'No,' she agreed. 'But I still felt responsible,

and stupid, and scared. Especially during the trial.'

His eyes searched her face. 'It must have been hard.'

Mimi swallowed. Thankfully, it was all a blur. There had been so much happening—so many changes in such a short time. Mostly it had felt like riding a rollercoaster—slow stretches of normality and then a sudden, plunging, terrifying dip.

'It was exhausting. And confusing. And we were so naïve—or maybe I was naïve. My mum was just out of it.'

'What do you mean by naïve?'

'I mean stupid. Dopey.'

She bit her lip, remembering the first time a news story about her had popped up on her phone. It had been like the kind of dream in which you're naked in public—except she had been awake, and there had been nowhere to hide.

'I knew it would be bad for Charlie and Raymond. I just never thought me and my mum would be on trial too. But we were, and we didn't have a barrister to speak for us.'

She looked across the lake to where a bunch of ducks and swans were mobbing a smaller bird.

'I hated those photographers. They were so insistent, so bullying. But it was never knowing how people were going to be that was the worst.' Her smile felt as if it was made of *papier-mâché*. 'Sometimes they'd be nice to my face, then talk about me behind my back, and other times they just crossed the street really pointedly.'

His jaw hardened. 'I'm sorry.'

'It's not your fault.'

'I didn't exactly help, though, did I?' He stared down at her, his dark gaze fixed on her face. 'And now? How is it now? Is it better?'

The genuineness of his concern made her feel a little dizzy. 'Most of the time.'

They were back at the house now, and as she gazed across the deck, she searched for the right words.

'I guess if it hadn't happened I would have argued more with the lawyers about my film. But I didn't want to risk someone working out who I am and going to the newspapers.' She met his gaze. 'Like you said, trust is hard to recover once it's lost.'

'But your life is okay?'

He seemed tense again, and her heart began to pound. Just for a moment she had felt a connection beyond the sexual—a shared understanding of the burden of guilt and responsibility. Now, though, he seemed on edge again, and she didn't understand why.

'Yes, it's fine. I live at home, and that's okay for now. I have a job I hate, but I like my colleagues, and I have Alicia.'

His eyes were steady and unblinking.

'Alicia thinks you deserve more. She thinks you need a man in your life.'

'Alicia's in love.' She managed to laugh. 'Of course she thinks that.'

'But you don't?'

She felt a rush of panic at both the dark intensity of his gaze and the unedited answer hovering dangerously on the tip of her tongue, like a swimmer poised on the high-dive board.

'I don't really think about it,' she lied.

She thought about it a lot. Even before her teenage crush on Basa she'd worried about whether she would ever be able to sustain a loving relationship, or if she would mess it up. The thought made her entire body grow tense.

'Look, I know Alicia wants me to have what she has, but I haven't met anyone I want to be with in that way...' She stumbled over the lie. 'And I don't want my first time to be with some random man...'

She froze, and there was a long, pulsing silence as her words echoed loudly back and forth across the still stretch of water.

'Your first time?' He frowned. 'What do you mean *your first time*?'

Her heart was pounding and she could feel the blood rushing to her face.

'Are you saying you haven't had sex with anyone?'

She pulled her hand away, flustered as much by his sudden intense focus as by her slip of the tongue. 'It doesn't matter.'

'It doesn't matter...?'

He sounded confused, and she felt more panic, followed by a rush of irritation.

'Yes, Basa, it doesn't matter.'

'It matters to me.'

'Why would it? Oh, right.' She stopped

abruptly. 'I get it. You didn't believe me yesterday.'

'That's not true. I did believe you.'

'So why the shocked expression?'

His dark gaze narrowed. 'I don't know... maybe because you said all that stuff about sampling new flavours.'

She felt her face grow hot. It was true, she had—but only so as not to lose face.

'Why would you lie about that?' His mouth tightened.

'My sex life was...*is* none of your business. And, frankly, I don't see how my being a virgin then or now has any effect on this.' She couldn't keep the shake out of her voice. 'Unless in some mad way you think being one makes me some kind of innocent?'

'No, of course I'm not saying that.' His eyes narrowed. 'I'm saying that you being a virgin changes the facts, and if you'd just told me that, right at the beginning at that stupid lunch with Alicia and Philip, we wouldn't have had to go through all of this.'

A red veil was slipping in front of her face. Was he blaming *her* for his actions? 'That's not fair...' The injustice of his words felt like a blow to the head. 'You didn't want to listen to anything I had to say.'

'Oh, I promise you, Mimi, if you'd told me that I would have listened.'

'Okay, maybe you would.' Her pulse was dancing with indignation. 'But you wouldn't have believed me, would you?'

He didn't reply, but she felt no satisfaction at having been proved right. Instead, she was feeling slightly sick—and trapped.

'So now you know everything there is to know about me, Basa,' she lied, 'so this conversation is officially over.'

Spinning around, she walked quickly back into the house, wanting to get as far away as possible from the truth that had followed her halfway around the world. Not the fact that she was a virgin, but the fact that he didn't trust her and never would.

Watching her leave, Basa felt his whole body tense. He'd made such a mess of this. And he couldn't blame Mimi. Although, true to form, he had done exactly that.

He breathed out unsteadily, a splinter of guilt stabbing between his ribs. It had never occurred to him that she might still be a virgin and her admission had caught him off balance. He'd felt angry with her for not telling him, so it had been easy to blame her for making him act irrationally.

But really he was angry and disgusted with himself.

For not bothering to check her level of experience and not letting her give her side of the story.

For not completely believing that she had been a virgin that night.

And for blaming her for his own selfish and shoddy behaviour.

Without realising it he was walking through the house, driven by a sense of purpose he hadn't felt since the morning after Alicia's birthday party.

He was going to make this right. And he was going to do it now.

He caught up with her just outside her bedroom door.

'Mimi—'

'I don't want to talk any more, Basa.' She

stepped into her room, holding up her hand to halt him.

'I know, but I have to say this—please, Mimi.'

He watched her hand tremble as she lowered it.

'You were right. I didn't completely believe you and I'm sorry for that—I'm sorry for all of this. I brought you here to prove I was right about you. But I wasn't. I was wrong.' He breathed out unsteadily. 'And you were right about me. I never gave you a chance. I ignored everything Alicia said about you because it was easier—'

Her blue eyes widened. 'What do you mean?'

He hesitated. It was a secret he'd always kept to himself: that the shock of Charlie and Raymond's betrayal had hurt less than believing Mimi hadn't wanted him that night.

'That night at Fairbourne I wanted you so badly it hurt, and I thought you wanted me.'

'I did,' she said shakily.

'I know.' He corrected himself. 'I know that *now*. But that night I thought you'd played me. And then, when everything came out, I was so angry with you, with myself, I let that anger blank out everything else. Only, this is not who

I am, Mimi, and I'm ashamed of myself for behaving like this. I'm so sorry if the way I acted that night put you off getting involved with anyone else.'

She was staring at him, her face framed in the light from the window.

'It didn't. Not in the way you mean. I could have had sex with other men, but I didn't want to because…' She hesitated. 'Because none of them made me feel the way you did just by looking at me.' Her mouth trembled. 'The way you still make me feel.'

His heart seemed to have doubled in size. 'Do you mean that?'

His pulse jumped as she nodded slowly.

He lifted his hand and gently caressed her cheek. 'I haven't been able to get you out of my head,' he said softly.

Her eyes widened. 'Really?'

Staring down into her face, he nodded. 'Really. I wish I'd said something sooner, but mostly I wish I'd done this…'

Capturing her head, he lowered his mouth and kissed her lightly, moving his lips across hers, his body hardening as he heard her breath catch in her throat.

* * *

Mimi felt her stomach clench with need. Her head was spinning. His lips were soft but firm, and he smelled of clean air and beech leaves. He was all she'd ever wanted—but she'd been here before and it was hard to forget how it had ended.

She felt her body stiffen at the memory of those long minutes of waiting for him to return.

'It's okay.'

Sensing her hesitation, he broke the kiss, his dark gaze searching her face.

'It's just a kiss,' he said soothingly.

'I don't want it to be just a kiss. But I don't want it to go wrong again.'

'Easy…' He pulled her closer, cupping her face. 'It won't go wrong. But there's no rush. Do you need time to think?'

'I've had time.' Shakily, she reached out and rested her hand on his chest, feeling the swift, unsteady beat of his heart. 'A long time. And I want to make love with you. Here. Now.'

His breathing jerked and she felt his heart accelerate beneath her palm.

'I want that too,' he said hoarsely.

His gaze slid slowly down her body and then

he began to kiss her again, nudging her gently back towards the bed, his fingers slipping under her top, sliding over her skin, slow and soft and sure.

'Okay?'

He lifted his face to hers and she nodded. Then, with fingers trembling, she pressed her hand against the hard push of his erection. He sucked in a breath and her stomach clenched at his obvious hunger for her, at the size of him. How could she give this man what he needed?

He caught her hand with his, his breathing unsteady as his eyes met hers. 'Don't be scared. I won't let it hurt. I don't ever want to hurt you.'

'I'm not scared…just a bit nervous.'

'So let me help you relax,' he said softly.

He stripped off his clothes, and then hers, gently peeling off her bra and panties, kissing her the whole time, his hands caressing her hip, her waist, the underside of her breast, until she was shaking with need, wanting him to touch the fluttering pulse between her thighs.

When they were both naked she felt her stomach tighten with nerves. He was so solid and aroused, and his dark gaze was so intense she could feel it deep inside her.

'Why are you looking at me like that?'

'You're beautiful.'

Saliva pooling in her mouth, she stared at his lean, beautifully muscled body, her eyes lingering on the smooth length of his erection.

'So are you,' she said softly.

He smiled, and she smiled back at him, and then she felt her whole body start to throb as he pulled her gently towards the bed.

His skin was just as she remembered it—smooth and warm and firm. Greedily, she caressed the contours of his back, her breathing losing its rhythm as his hands dropped to her waist. He pressed her against the thick ridge of his erection and she felt her heartbeat accelerate in time with the oscillating ball of heat low in her pelvis.

He began moving against her slowly, his hot mouth seeking the bare skin of her neck, kissing and licking the raised line of her clavicle until she was drowning in the dark, teasing currents surging through her body.

She gasped as his hands caressed her eager, straining body, her head swimming as they slid over her ribcage to capture her breasts. His fingertips skimmed over her taut nipples, and then her stomach clenched sharply as those same fingers slipped down to the triangle of blonde hair and the slick heat between her thighs. His breathing jerked and she parted her legs, letting him take the weight of her in his hand, moving against the insistent press of his palm.

'I want you,' she whispered, her hand closing around him.

He groaned against her throat. 'Wait a minute,' he muttered.

She watched dazedly as he reached for his trousers and pulled out his wallet.

'Are you sure you want this?' He was holding a condom packet, but loosely, and she knew he was waiting for her consent. 'Are you sure you want me?' he said hoarsely.

She nodded. 'I've never been surer.'

And suddenly he was there, his big body warm and solid against hers. She locked her hands around his neck as he shifted against her, lowering his hips to hers, his erection hard and hot. And then her pulse accelerated as he pushed forward.

She took a breath, trying to relax, but her face must have given her away because he stopped moving.

'Don't stop,' she whispered.

'I'm just letting you get used to me.'

She felt his hand slide to her hip, shifting beneath her to raise her up, and suddenly it was easier, smoother. Now her body was welcoming him, and she was rising up to meet his thrusts.

Letting her arms curl around his shoulders, she pressed up against him, breath quickening, muscles clenching as a pulsing heat gathered inside her and exploded like a supernova, and then she felt him clamp her closer, his body erupting into hers with a groan.

CHAPTER EIGHT

BREATHING OUT UNSTEADILY, Mimi buried her
hands in Basa's dark hair, her heart racing in
time with his, lost in the aftershocks still quivering through her body, in the scent of his skin,
and in disbelief at her own uninhibited passion.

No one had ever held her like this…so close.

If only they could stay like this for ever.

She felt him shift against her and her heart
gave a little jump as he raised himself up onto
his elbows and stared down into her flushed
face.

'Was it okay?' He stroked her tangled blonde
hair away from her forehead.

She nodded, then smiled. 'It was a lot better
than okay.'

Something flared in his dark eyes. He lowered his mouth and she arched upwards as his
lips brushed her neck, her collarbone, the curve
of her breast.

Raising his head, he gently eased himself out of her. 'I'll be right back.'

Pulling the rumpled sheet up over her legs, she watched him walk into the bathroom, her breath catching in her throat. Earlier, she'd been too caught up with nerves and expectation and desire to take in his beauty, but he really was absolutely gorgeous, she thought, her eyes running down his spine to the muscular swell of his buttocks.

Rolling onto her side, she buried her face in the pillow, inhaling the faint trace of his after-shave. She felt stunned, happy, her body soft and loosened. She was suffused with a tranquillity very different from the sharp, sweet spasm of pleasure that had so recently swamped her, and she lay for a moment, trying to remember how she had felt before.

Did she feel different?

Her mind was still hazy from climaxing and it took a moment for her to bring order to her thoughts.

Yes and no.

Physically, she ached a little, but there had been no actual pain, just a sense of being stretched—and, frankly, her head had been spinning, her body rippling with other more urgent and pleasurable sensations for her to register the actual moment.

And yet she did feel different—though not because of some shift in status to 'full womanhood'. Maybe she would have had that kind of transformative moment if she'd still been an adolescent, but for her this was not just about having sex for the first time...it was about what it felt like to surrender, truly surrender, to desire. It was about discovering a different side to herself—a passionate and fearless self so unlike the woman who had been living her life in the shadows for the last two years.

It had felt so right, beginning her sexual awakening with Basa. But not out of any lingering, sentimental attachment to her teenage fantasies—that fairy-tale prince of her dreams had never existed except in her imagination.

The man who was here with her now was not perfect at all. He was stubborn, and ruthless, but he was also loyal and caring and he had a deep-rooted sense of responsibility for his family, friends, and employees. Most importantly of all, he was real, and together the two of them had faced their shared past, here in this beautiful wilderness.

She glanced out of the window. The sun was shining, birds were singing—everything was carrying on without any thought of what had just happened in this room.

What would happen next?

Her breath swelled in her throat. It was stupid, really. She'd spent so many years dreaming about Basa and it was only now she realised that her fantasy had stopped at the moment of climax.

Her eyes darted towards the discarded clothes on the floor. Was he going to come out of the bathroom and just start getting dressed? She sat up. Should *she* be getting dressed?

Before she had a chance to move he walked back into the room and slid in beside her, gathering her against him.

Her heart rebounded inside her chest and she breathed in against a rush of emotions. But it was okay to feel a little emotional, she told herself. It was her first time, and the sex had been so good; Basa had made it good for her.

For a moment she lay listening to his breathing, savouring the heat and solidity of his body next to hers, and then she turned and looked up at him. 'How about you? Was it okay for you?'

He stared at her for a moment. 'It was a whole lot better than okay.' His face softened, and he laughed. 'Do you know, nobody has ever asked me that before?'

She laughed too. 'There's a first time for everything.'

'Yes, there is.' He touched her cheek gently, his face growing more serious. 'Did you mean what you said about why you waited?'

When she nodded slowly, he dipped his head and kissed her, his hand hugging the curve of her hip.

'I really am sorry, Mimi, for how that evening ended between us, and for leaving you up in my room like that.'

'It doesn't matter any more.'

'But it did then,' he persisted. 'And I think it's stayed with you.'

She was about to tell him it hadn't, only she didn't want to lie to him any more. 'A bit,' she confessed.

She hesitated, the impulse to make light of her feelings fighting with her need to be truthful.

'But I can't blame how I felt entirely on what happened at Fairbourne.'

A minute ticked by and then he frowned. 'What do you mean?'

She felt suddenly aware of his gaze, and of the pulse beating in her throat.

'There were things before that. Like my parents. They had an incredibly passionate relationship and I wasn't planned.'

Body tensing, she took a shallow breath. It was the first time she'd told anyone that—not even Alicia knew—and it made her feel horribly exposed.

'I wasn't either. Apparently my father was astonished when my mother told him.'

He spoke matter-of-factly and, looking up, she felt some of the tightness ease from her shoulders.

'My dad was astonished too—but not in a good way.' She dropped her gaze. 'Me being around changed things—for my dad anyway. He left, and my mum never really got over it. That's why I was so happy when she and Charlie got together.'

His face stiffened, but it was too late to take it back.

She swallowed. 'Actually, I wasn't just happy… I encouraged her.'

She held her breath, expecting to see contempt or confusion in his eyes.

But after a moment he said quietly, 'For the right reasons.'

'I suppose…'

His words had made warmth snake across her skin, and for a few quivering seconds she wanted to tell him more. But surely it was better to quit while she was ahead, so instead she shrugged.

'Anyway, I got on with my life, and you had a good reason for not coming back to me that night.'

He hadn't told her much, but it was easy to embellish the bare bones he'd given her—the nightmarish hours following that call to his lawyer, his escalating shock and disbelief at each emerging revelation.

'I don't know how you dealt with all of it,' she said quietly. 'You were so young.' Just twenty-seven. 'But you took care of everything…you righted the wrongs.'

'Not all of them,' he said softly.

His fingers twitched against her skin. Leaning forward, he caught a handful of her hair and wrapped it around his fingers, using it to draw her closer to him. She felt her insides grow liquid and hot as he stared down into her face, his breath warm against her skin.

'But I'm planning on making up for lost time.'

'You are?' Her voice sounded far away, muffled by the uneven thud of her heartbeat.

'If you want me to.'

She could feel her body rippling back to life as his dark gaze roamed her face. He was answering her unasked question, offering her a next step. What should she say?

He was talking about sex, and though she wanted to make up for lost time as much as he did, she couldn't help but be a little nervous. She didn't need to ask, didn't *want* to ask about his previous partners, but it was clear that Basa was sexually experienced—certainly experienced enough to be able to separate his emotions from his libido.

But how did she know she could do the same?

She'd only had sex once, and maybe if it *had* been just 'okay' then it would have been easy to walk away—to treat this as a one-off, her first and last time with Basa. Maybe if it *had* been just 'okay' she would honestly have said that sex was just a physical activity, involving bodies.

But sex with Basa had been astonishing, frantic, miraculous. And, although her one experience hardly qualified her as an expert, she knew already that for her it had been more than just bodies moving in time with one another. There had been tenderness, and with tenderness came vulnerability, and she was already vulnerable enough where Basa was concerned. She wasn't sure if she would be able to stop herself from making the physical attraction between them more than it really was, and yet…

His skin felt so deliciously warm and smooth, and she couldn't resist running a hand over his stomach, her fingers tracing the contoured lines of his muscles, her head dizzy with the freedom of being able to reach out and touch him, of not having to hold herself in check.

He sucked in a breath, his hand catching hers.

'What's the matter?' She looked up at him.

'Nothing.' He shook his head. 'I'm trying to play it cool here, but my body's acting like it belongs to some horny teenager.'

The air between them seemed to thicken, and

her pulse quickened at his confession, at his open acknowledgement of her power to arouse him.

'I thought you wanted to make up for lost time?' she said softly.

Her hand slid lower down over his belly, trembling slightly, and she wrapped her fingers around his hard, straining length, her breathing losing its rhythm as his pupils flared.

'Oh, I do,' he said hoarsely as he reached out and cupped her breast, his thumb brushing lightly, maddeningly, across her rigid nipple.

Somewhere low down and deep inside she could feel herself melting, and she squirmed against his hand, moaning softly. She felt his breathing change as he pulled her close and rolled onto his back, taking her with him, anchoring her aching, hollowed-out body to his with not quite steady hands.

Shivering, she arched, pressing down against him as his fingers caressed her breasts, their teasing touch sending ripples through her body so that she could think of nothing but him, nothing but her need to feel his heat and power again, to feel him inside her.

She shifted against him, parting her legs further, chasing the fluttering beat of heat that was just out of reach. Groaning, he leaned sideways, fumbling on the floor for his discarded wallet, his other hand gripping her against him.

'Here.'

He handed her the condom packet and she tore it open.

'Pinch the end.'

His jaw was clenched, the muscles bunching in his arms as she rolled it onto his hard length. She felt a wet heat flood between her thighs at the barely checked hunger in his eyes, and then she lowered herself onto the blunt head of his erection.

His fingers grazed her stomach, strangling the breath in her throat.

'Don't be scared,' he whispered, sliding his hands under her bottom and lifting her up. 'Just take it slow. I won't move until you're—'

He breathed in sharply as she reached down and took him in her hand, guiding him slowly. A moan climbed up her throat as she pushed down, her body stretching, filling with what she wanted. His fingers reached for her breasts and then, raising himself up, he took first one and then the other nipple into his mouth, tonguing and licking them in turn, his breathing ragged as she started to rock against him.

Her body was contracting, tightening and pulsing around him, and then he started to move beneath her. She was moving in time with him, torn between the soft press of his mouth and the hard push of his body.

He made a rough sound and fell back against the pillow, his dark eyes resting on her face. His hands moved over her thighs, and then between them, his fingers oscillating in time to her heartbeat until she was shaking with need and pleasure.

'Look at me, Mimi,' he whispered.

She stared down into his face, her breath jerking from her throat as he eased himself in and out of her body with ever-increasing urgency. His hands gripped her waist and she cried out, her body splintering apart, gripping him tightly as he groaned and thrust up inside her.

Her heartbeat was filling her head and she shuddered against him as he breathed out unevenly, his chest rising and falling. Heart pounding, she stared down at him, trying to imprint the moment into her memory, wanting to remember the shape of his mouth, the pull of his gaze, the feel of his body inside hers.

'Come here.' Pulling her forward, he kissed her, and then, cupping her face, pressed his forehead against hers. 'You're smiling,' he said softly.

Mimi tilted her head back. 'I'm happy.'

Happier than she could ever remember being. Except she couldn't help but feel a flicker of apprehension—because in her world happiness came with an inbuilt risk that at some unspecified point in the future all of it could be taken away.

His eyes were dark and unwavering. 'What a coincidence. So am I.'

Pulling her closer, he smiled, and instantly she forgot her fears and was lost in his smile, lost in him, so that nothing mattered except the press of his lips against hers...

Basa shifted forward in his chair. As he scrolled down his laptop screen he tried to concentrate on what his PA had written. Rebecca was an excellent PA, and normally he enjoyed her concise and meticulous reports, but today he was struggling to focus on anything other than the woman standing on the deck outside his window.

Mimi was staring across the lake. She was holding up some kind of video camera, so he couldn't see her face. She was wearing nothing that could be described as even vaguely attention-seeking, and yet his gaze kept returning to her approximately every ten seconds.

Sighing, he closed his laptop and leaned back, frowning at his uncharacteristic lack of focus. On an average day he would have worked through a report like this one in a couple of hours, and his recommendations would already be winging their way back to Rebecca.

Only this wasn't an average day. It was the day he and Mimi had become lovers and he was still coming to terms with that new and incredible reality.

His pulse jumped. He was Mimi's first lover, and he was a little confused—ashamed, even— by how much that mattered to him. He'd always thought of himself as modern and urbane, but against his will—against that image of himself—he could feel himself liking the fact that he was her first.

He breathed out slowly. It felt weird not to

recognise his feelings—but why should his feelings be immune to change? Over the last forty-eight hours he and Mimi had more or less rewritten their shared history, and it appeared that he'd spent the last two years spectacularly misjudging her in about as many ways as it was possible to misjudge a person.

Remembering her remark about the view from his high horse, he felt his mouth twist. That horse had bucked him off—big-time.

A movement out on the deck tugged at his gaze and he glanced over. His eyes narrowed and his body hardened with crashing predictability at the sight of Mimi leaning over the table. She was obviously just playing around with angles, as she had been doing most of the morning, but thanks to the feverish desire gripping his body it took less than thirty seconds for his brain to summon up a vision of her leaning in much the same way over his bed... wearing nothing but those heels she'd had on in the restaurant...

Breathing in sharply, he stood up. He needed to move—get some fresh air, get some perspective. Or at least stop what Alicia would call objectifying women.

Alicia.

He gritted his teeth. He had completely forgotten about his sister in all this, but now he felt his chest tighten. He was fairly sure he knew how Alicia would react. With her wedding so close, she was predictably loved-up right now, and he could imagine that nothing would give her greater happiness than for her brother and best friend to fall in love.

Except they weren't in love.

In lust, definitely—but love? That feeling of being intertwined with someone else's essence? That was something he had never felt.

Of course in a perfect world he would choose what Alicia had with Philip, what his parents had shared for twenty-two years. But it was the aftermath of his mother's tragic death, not his parents' happy life together, that he remembered the most.

In the weeks and months following the accident all their lives had been knocked off course. Alicia had been just fourteen, and she had been devastated, but his father had never recovered from losing the woman he loved, and for a time it had felt as if they were orphans.

He'd hated seeing his sister so upset and his

father so broken. All he'd wanted to do was take away their pain, to protect them from a cruel and unjust world, and now he wanted to do the same for Mimi.

He could protect her here. Here, they were safe—*she* was safe—from the predatory press and a public hungry for gossip.

But they couldn't stay on this island for ever.

He glanced down at his laptop. Back in the real world he had responsibilities—a business to run, a family who needed him. What was happening here with Mimi wasn't real, and it wouldn't—couldn't—survive any kind of brush with reality.

And yet this thing with Mimi felt more real than any relationship he'd ever had, and although it might sound crazy he felt closer to her than to all the other women he'd dated.

But was it that surprising?

One way or another Mimi had been in his life for the best part of a decade.

And now she was in his bed.

Only, what did that mean?

For him? For her? For both of them?

It was a question he'd been asking himself in a variety of ways since leaving her bedroom, and he was still no closer to answering it. But maybe he didn't actually need to know what any of it meant when they would both be back in England tomorrow.

Ignoring the tension in his back at that thought, he made his way outside.

On the deck, Mimi was now talking to Claudia. There was nothing remarkable about that, except the fact she was speaking in Spanish. Agreed, she was not particularly fluent, but he found it oddly endearing that she was bothering. In fact, he was surprised that her making such an effort mattered so much to him.

He stopped beside her. *'Muy impresionante!'*

Turning she blushed. *'Gracias...* I think.'

He felt his own skin prickle as she met his gaze. 'I didn't know you spoke Spanish.'

'That would be because I don't.' She turned to the housekeeper, smiling. 'As Claudia can confirm.'

Claudia shook her head. 'I was the same as you when I started speaking English. What is important is to try.'

From the direction of the kitchen a buzzer went off, and she excused herself and went back into the house.

For a moment neither of them spoke, and the silence was broken only by the gentle rhythmic splash of water against the side of the deck.

After the fierce intensity of their naked coupling it felt strange seeing her clothed, out here in the daylight, and he could tell from her stillness that his feelings mirrored hers.

His mind rewound an hour, his blood beating hot and fast as he remembered how she had felt and tasted, her lack of inhibition, her curiosity and hunger. Before today he would have said that sex was just sex, for typically the hunger that possessed him passed as quickly as early-morning mist when it was satisfied, but with Mimi the opposite seemed to be true, and instead of fading his body was still hard and aching.

He looked down at her. She looked so young, so wary, and he felt the ache of guilt at the part he had personally played in robbing her of her confidence. It might not have been intentional but, whatever she had said earlier, he could tell from the tension in her shoulders that she was waiting for things to fall apart.

He felt a sudden need to reassure her, to re-build her trust in people. In him. There had been too much confusion between them, too many lies in her life already, so he needed to be honest.

He hesitated before taking hold of her hand and pulling her closer. 'Are you still happy?'

Her blue eyes were searching his face.

'Yes, but…' She paused. 'I don't know how this part works.'

'I don't know either,' he said softly. Watching her frown, he shrugged. 'I like women, and I like sex, but the aftermath is not my thing. Usually I have a reason to leave—or I create one.' Lifting her hand to his mouth, he kissed the palm. 'But I'm not ready to leave just yet, and I thought you might not be either, only—'

His pulse twitched. Since when had he decided on extending his stay? Or asking Mimi to join him?

She blinked. 'Only what?'

'Only I didn't give you much choice about coming out to Argentina, and no choice whatsoever about coming all the way out here. I was out of order, and I'm sorry for how I acted.'

She bit her lip. 'It *was* out of order, but I can understand now why you did it. You had your reasons, and you were right.' She held his gaze. 'We did need to talk.'

'And now we have…so theoretically there's no reason for us to stay any more.' He stared down into her eyes. 'I guess what I'm asking is do you want to go back to England? Or do you think you might have a reason to stay for a couple more days?'

He could almost follow her thoughts, fear battling with longing.

'I don't know if that's a good idea.' She hesitated. 'But I really want to make this wedding film sing, and if I had more time here I think that would help me get a feel for what will work best. But I suppose I just need to know what's happening…' A flush of pink suffused her cheeks. 'With us, I mean—'

His heart kicked against his ribs. At least one of them was being honest. He stared at her in silence, fighting against the protective feeling produced by her words, concentrating on the facts. It had taken guts to ask that question—more guts than he had, apparently—so the least he could do was be brave enough to answer it.

Pulling her closer, he smoothed her hair back from her face. 'It's simple, really. I want you and you want me. We both know it's not permanent, but that doesn't mean it's not real, Mimi.' He took a slow breath, recalling his earlier thoughts. 'And it *is* real for me—as real as you are, here in my arms.'

She nodded. 'For me, too.'

His heart beat faster—not just with desire but relief. 'So will you stay?'

She hesitated, then nodded again.

Lowering his mouth to hers, he kissed her quickly, closing his eyes to block out the uncertainty in hers. He didn't do love and he couldn't love Mimi. She was too young, too much of a responsibility, and he already had enough responsibilities to last a lifetime. He could never truly right the wrongs of the past—his or anyone else's—but she deserved to be happy, and for the next few days he was going to do everything in his power to make that happen.

'Where are we going?'

Frowning, Mimi glanced over to where Basa sat beside her, his dark hair blowing in the wind. One of his staff, Lionel, was driving them up a bumpy and quite steep grassy hillside, and she was having to grip both the underside of her seat and Basa's hand, just to stop herself from sliding sideways.

Turning, he squeezed her hand. 'It's not far now.'

'That doesn't answer my question,' she complained.

He smiled, and as she watched his lips curve upwards her heart felt too big for her ribs and her question seemed suddenly irrelevant.

'I don't want to risk spoiling the surprise,' he said.

'It would have been a lot easier choosing what to wear if you'd given me a clue,' she grumbled. 'Now I don't know if I'm underdressed or overdressed.'

His dark eyes rested on her face, then dropped over the curve of her breasts beneath her wrap top. 'As far as I'm concerned if you're not naked then you're overdressed.'

Mimi felt her skin grow warm. She still found his hunger for her incredibly exciting, and just thinking about his hands and mouth exploring her naked body made her mouth turn dry. The last two days had passed with incredible speed, and this was their final morning in Patagonia. Basa had woken her before the sun had even risen and her body had instantly softened in response.

But he'd rolled them both out of bed and dragged her into the shower.

She'd felt disappointed...a little crushed, actually...until he'd pulled her closer, and kissed her fiercely. Then he'd dropped to his knees and she'd felt his hands grip her hips before he'd started kissing the tops of her legs.

Her breath fluttered in her throat as she remembered the feel of his flickering tongue as it had eased between her thighs, nudging against the tight ball of heat there, his warm saliva mixing with the warm water.

She'd had no idea that she would feel as if her actual bones were melting, and afterwards, when he'd gently turned her away from him and thrust into her, his arm around her waist, anchoring her to his body, she had felt both his power and his tenderness.

Now, pressing her knees together, she glanced over at Basa's profile. She couldn't imagine any other man being so expert, so fierce, so generous—couldn't imagine being with another man. But that would change, she told herself.

It would have to change. And at least this way there was no time for her to mess it up.

As they reached the top of the hill the ground flattened and she saw there was another car already parked. Two men were leaning against the car, and spread out over the springy grass was a huge pale blue and white hot air balloon.

She swallowed a breath.

'We haven't left the island since you got here, and I can't let you go back to England without seeing something of my second homeland,' Basa said quietly. 'This way you'll get to see so much more.'

The thought of going back to England made her chest feel too tight, and suddenly her eyes were burning with tears.

But she smiled past the ache in her throat. 'I've always wanted to do this…'

His eyes held hers. 'So let's go sail along the silver sky. Here—' he handed her a quilted jacket '—you'll need this.'

It took thirty minutes to inflate the balloon. Their pilot, Butch, spoke very good English, but with a strong Spanish accent.

Mimi frowned as Basa helped her into the basket. 'Butch isn't a very Argentinian name.'

Butch laughed. 'My real name is Gonzalo, but everyone calls me Butch because I am from Cholila.'

'Cholila is outlaw country,' Basa explained. 'Butch Cassidy and the Sundance Kid hid out there for a while when they were on the run.' His eyes hovered over the pulse-point in her throat. 'Since Butch is in charge, for this ride at least, maybe that makes you and me outlaws too.'

His smile transfixed her, slowed her pulse and stilled all thought, so that it was perhaps a full five minutes before she realised that the balloon was slowly rising up.

Her head began to spin. Basa had been right. The sky was silver up here—and blue and pink and gold. The air was crisp, but the rising sun was warm, and then Basa wrapped his arms around her waist and the heat of his body quickly enveloped her.

'There's the island,' he said, leaning in, his cheek brushing against her.

'Look at the lake—it's so blue.'

From so high, the translucent water was jewel-bright, studded with the dark shapes of ducks and swans. Heart thumping, she gazed down. Beneath them she could see grazing cattle, and Basa pointed out an eagle soaring in the air currents. It was so vast, so open, with huge, grassy plains spreading in every direction, right up to the foothills of the mountains, and all of it was gilded in sunlight.

She turned to look at him, a painful heat filling her chest. 'Alicia said you call this place the first step to heaven.'

'I do.' His eyes, dark like the rocks in the lake, met hers. 'And now I have my very own angel.'

Was it the poetry of his words making her feel so dizzy? Or the fact that he wanted to share this beautiful place with her even for a moment? She didn't know, but it was a bittersweet feeling to remember that tomorrow this would all be just a memory.

Her heart felt as though it was being squeezed. She thought she had known loss and sadness, but this was a new kind of feeling—an emptiness that made her feel as if she was hollow inside. Her hand gripped the side of the basket. Her pulse was pounding, and she was torn between wanting to capture this moment for ever—his face, his voice, the way he filled not just the basket but this endless sky—and forgetting they had ever met.

The rest of the flight seemed to pass in seconds, and then Butch brought them down with little more than a bump. Within minutes the two SUVs were powering through the grass towards them.

Back at the house, she spent the rest of the day trying to ignore the ache that had started inside her up in the silvery sky. She packed, and talked and smiled with Claudia, and watched Lionel build a vast willow frame above a circle of fire for an *asado* later.

And then she and Basa walked around the island until the ache became unbearable and she was suddenly frantic for the feel of his body on hers, and in hers, and she towed him back to the bedroom where they made love for the rest of the afternoon.

Later, they sat by the fire, drinking ice-cold champagne while Lionel and Claudia cooked the meat.

'What you were talking about earlier,' he said abruptly. 'About you not being planned by your parents. I don't understand what my not coming back to the room that night has to do with the way that made you feel.'

For a moment her mind was utterly blank, but then, as she tried to think of a way to answer his question, she felt something stir inside her. When they made love they held nothing back, so why was she still hiding herself from him?

'Sometimes it feels like it's my fault,' she said carefully. 'That if I hadn't been born my parents would still be together.'

'Maybe they weren't meant to be together.'

She wanted to believe him, and she was sure he believed what he was saying, but he only knew some of the facts.

'I mess things up.' Her mouth began to tremble and she twisted it into a mangled smile. 'Not just my parents' marriage. I messed up with you. And the film I made has never been seen by anyone except lawyers.'

'You didn't mess up with me. It was just as much my fault as yours. And whatever those lawyers are arguing, I bet I could find ten different lawyers to say the opposite.'

Suddenly there were tears in her eyes. 'It wouldn't make any difference,' she said wearily. *'I'm* the problem. I ruin everything.'

'Not everything,' he said gently.

She felt her heart contract. He was being so sweet, and she was ruining their last night together. With an effort she smiled up at him. 'No, not everything.'

It was getting dark by the time the food was ready, and they ate greedily, licking the meat juices from their fingers. There was also trout from the lake, whole squashes and potatoes cooked in the ashes, and for dessert slow-roasted peaches that seemed to melt in her mouth.

'Like it?'

Mimi looked up. Basa was watching her, his face half in darkness, his eyes like stars.

She nodded. 'It's amazing. It's all amazing.'

He was amazing.

She had thought he was cold-hearted and judgmental, but she knew now that he was neither. He was kind and loyal and strong, and the idea of being apart from him for even a day was unbearable.

All of a sudden she felt dizzy—the same dizziness she had felt in the balloon, when she'd been trying to commit Basa to memory.

Only, there had been no need. Her heart had

got there first. She didn't have to try and re-member him. She already knew everything about him by heart—the good and the bad—and that was why she loved him.

For a moment she sat gazing across the dark stretch of water, stunned by the truth. In a few short days he had become not just familiar, but necessary to her life. It was new and thrilling to feel like this, and yet so old, for she had never really stopped loving him. Why else had she agreed to come out to Argentina in the first place?

She wanted to tell him. To share her feelings. After all they had shared everything else: their bodies, their fears, their anger and pain. And now their love?

Except it wasn't *their* love, it was only *hers*, in spite of the intensity of their lovemaking and the romantic appearance of these last few days.

She knew all about Basa's deep-seated sense of responsibility for those around him, his need to right the wrongs. And that was all she was to him—a wrong to be righted.

The ache in her chest was spreading and, needing to make it stop, she leaned forward and took his face in her hands, kissing him fiercely.

'I need you,' she whispered.

And he pulled her to her feet and led her back into the house, where they stripped one another naked and she welcomed the wordless oblivion of her body's response to his.

CHAPTER NINE

GAZING DOWN INTO the lake, Basa stood shivering for a moment in the crisp morning air and then, tipping forward, he executed a perfect forward dive.

His heart jolted, and he felt the chill of the water like a punch. Striking out, he began to swim towards the distant shore. Normally he loved swimming in the lake—loved the sense of freedom and peace, the chance to connect with nature in its raw state—but today he just needed to move, to lose himself in the rhythm of his body and briefly suspend the conflicted thoughts that had dogged him since waking.

Last night had been incredible— He frowned. No, that was wrong. There were no words, or none in *his* vocabulary, to describe what it had been like, but he did know that it would never be as good with any other woman.

They had made love repeatedly, feverishly at first, with his body responding to the white heat of her desire and the urgency of her mouth, and then more slowly, each of them holding back, letting their hunger build in time with their accelerating heartbeats, neither one wanting that time to be the last, so that even before their shuddering bodies had stilled they were reaching for one another again.

He had fallen asleep with Mimi's body caught against his and woken early with a cramp in his arm. Shifting free, he had found it impossible to doze off again, with his body tuning in to the tension in his head, so he had quietly rolled off the bed, found his swim-shorts, and made his way onto the deck.

Slowing his stroke, he lifted his head from the water. He was more than halfway across the lake and his muscles were warm now, and aching. Using the glow from last night's *asado* as a beacon, he headed back towards the deck, his arms working in time with the arguments and counter-arguments firing back and forth.

Logically, he knew that he and Mimi had no future, and that the only reason it felt as if they did was the fact that they had been cooped up together with a barrel-load of heightened and complicated emotions and a shared history for company.

A shared history that was still mired in scandal…a scandal that definitely hadn't yet reached its sell-by date. And he couldn't risk exposing his family, or Mimi, to any more unwanted media attention.

His fingers grazed the wooden underside of the deck and, reaching up, he pulled himself out of the water, smoothing his wet hair back, feeling his skin burning in the cool air.

This time tomorrow his life would be back on track, he told himself. Okay it was going to feel a little odd, her not being there, but with the benefit of time and distance it would soon seem like nothing more than a fantasy frozen in time.

Only, having steeled himself to face a future without her, now he was floored by the reality of what that would mean.

He couldn't picture a bed without Mimi in it—and it wasn't just sex. He loved to lie and watch her brush her hair. Loved to hold her in his arms while they read to one another out loud from their books.

How could he walk away when every thought, every action came back to her?

Breathing out unevenly, he made his way back into the quiet of the house and to her room. She was still sleeping, and for a moment he stared down at her, his body loosening with desire, his heart pounding out of time, as he watched the steady rise and fall of her shoulders.

Then, as though sensing his presence, her eyes opened and she looked up at him drowsily. 'Basa...'

'I'm here.'

She shivered when he reached out and touched her bare collarbone, her eyes more grey than blue in the hazy morning light that was inching into the room. 'You're cold.'

'Sorry. I couldn't sleep, so I went for a swim in the lake. I'll go take a shower...warm up.'

'I've got a better idea.'

Her fingers slid up his thigh and his muscles bunched as she pressed her hand flat against the erection that was pushing against the damp fabric of his shorts.

'Come back to bed,' she whispered. 'Body-to-body heat is the best way to get warm.'

It wasn't heat he wanted—it was her. And not just to warm up his body. But what he wanted was complicated, fraught with risk.

He watched her slide his shorts down over his hips, and as he slipped beneath the sheets he let his hunger blot out everything else.

'Forgive me.' Switching off his phone, Basa ran his hand over his face, grimacing apologetically at Mimi. 'That was my head of HR in New York. She's been sitting on something for a few days now and I really needed to sign it off.'

They were on the plane now—somewhere over the North Atlantic. Both of them had slept on the overnight part of the flight, but since breakfast he had been trying to resolve this issue with his North American office.

Mimi looked up from her book and smiled. 'It's fine. It gave me an opportunity to get stuck into this.' Her blue eyes rested on his face and then dropped to the book in her lap. 'I'm nearly finished, so I should be able to give it back to you before we land. Or I can just give it to Alicia,' she added.

Her remark was innocuous enough, the kind

of polite comment anyone might make about a book they had borrowed, but he felt his body still, saw her still too, and knew that she had picked up on the unspoken implication of her words: when they stepped off the plane in London they would be going their separate ways.

'Keep it.' He managed to smile, his body tensing in ever-tightening anticipation of a moment he was dreading. 'Please, I'd like you to keep it.'

'Okay, well…thank you.' Looking up at him, she bit down on the corner of her lip. 'Was it a big problem? Your call?'

He shook his head. 'No, not really. It's a bit of a headache, but it's nothing major, and certainly nothing that can't be sorted. It's just that I have to be the one to sort it, and I don't normally drop off the grid so comprehensively.'

She frowned. 'But doesn't that happen every time you go to Patagonia?'

He held her gaze. 'No, actually, it doesn't. Usually, I crack and end up calling in.'

Her eyes narrowed. 'You told me there was no Wi-Fi.'

'There isn't,' he said quickly. 'But I do have a satellite phone.'

'That you forgot to mention?'

'No, I didn't forget. It was deliberate.' He sighed. 'In the beginning I didn't want you radioing home for back-up, and then later...'

He hesitated. Making love to Mimi and then sorting out this mess in New York had temporarily stifled the debate in his head over what he *should* do and what he *wanted* to do. He had done this journey so many times, and he knew that they were probably less than an hour away from landing. Now that they were so close to England he could no longer avoid the bruising reality of the facts.

If he didn't do or say something in the next sixty minutes then he was going to end up sleepwalking into a situation he didn't want— namely, Mimi's abrupt departure from his life.

But not from his head.

He felt his chest tighten, the impossibility of it all making his whole body tense with a panic he had never felt before.

When his mother had been killed he'd been too numb with shock to feel anything, and later the need to care for his sister and father had overwhelmed his own desperate loneliness and loss. And that night at Fairbourne when he'd called his lawyer had been the same. There had been no time to think about his own feelings; that had come later, after the dust had settled. And however terrible it had been—and it *had* been terrible—both times had been played out in public, shared with family and friends and police officers and lawyers.

This feeling was his alone, and he had to deal with it on his own.

His heart began to pound. It was an unsolvable dilemma. He and Mimi might work on an island on a lake in Patagonia, but they weren't outlaws. They couldn't run away and hide out at the edge of the world for ever.

Back in London—make that anywhere people had smartphones—his relationship with Mimi would be news, and once it was out there he wouldn't be able to control it.

He knew exactly how bad it might get. His body tensed as his mind recalled how bad it had been before. For a full year he hadn't been able to open a newspaper or search for his family's name on the internet without wanting to dig a hole and bury himself.

He couldn't unleash that kind of abuse on his loved ones.

'And then later, what?'

His head snapped up at the sound of Mimi's voice. He'd forgotten they were in the middle of a conversation, but now, looking down into her wide, blue eyes, he realised he was fighting a battle that had been lost the moment they had arrived on the island and given in to the inexorable sexual pull between them.

He took a breath. 'Then later... I didn't want you to leave.' Reaching out, he took her hand. 'I don't want you to leave now.'

Somehow saying it out loud made it more real, more urgent, and instantly he felt his mind refocus. He'd been thinking about this the wrong way—seeing their time together in Patagonia as an exception. But they didn't need an island to make this keep on working for however long it took for the fire between them to die. He had plenty of homes scattered across the globe, all of which were well protected from the public's curious gaze. Homes with high walls, large grounds and loyal staff, including well-trained and highly efficient security teams. With a little effort on both parts they could carry on just as before. All he needed to do was find out if Mimi was willing to make that effort.

'I don't want this to end. You and me…what we have. I thought you might come and stay at my townhouse…maybe we could talk it through.' He hesitated. 'I suppose what I'm trying to say is that I'm not ready to say goodbye just yet.'

For a moment the only sound in the cabin was the hum of the engine and the faint chatter of his crew, and then Mimi looked up at him, her mouth trembling.

'I'm not ready to say goodbye yet either.'

He pulled her against him, his mouth finding hers. There was a fullness in her chest, a relief that seemed stupid now she had agreed, but he couldn't stop himself from pulling her closer, then closer still, until there was no gap between them.

It was raining, and after the wide open skies of Patagonia, London felt like a toy town. Glancing up through the tinted glass at the grey English clouds, Mimi felt her stomach flip over. Since that moment during the flight, when Basa had told her that he wanted her to come and stay at his house, her emotions had been swirling inside her like a tornado. She was happy and scared, excited and stunned, and nervous—absurdly and acutely nervous.

Every time she opened her mouth she thought she was going to blurt it all out: her feelings, her love for him. She could feel it swelling up inside her, pulsing between them.

She clenched her hands in her lap. She loved him so much, but telling him would be an act of madness. He might have feelings for her, but he'd never so much as hinted that they were of a permanent or romantic variety, and him not wanting to say goodbye yet didn't change anything. What he was offering was merely an extension of their current arrangement, not a declaration of eternal love.

'What are you thinking?'

Her pulse jumped as Basa leaned over and put his hand on hers, pulling her fingers apart and then slotting them between his own.

She smiled. 'Everything feels so small.'

He nodded. 'I know. It's crazy, isn't it? Thirteen million people live in London, but right now it feels like a village.'

His dark eyes rested on her face, his mouth curving up into a smile that made her forget to breathe.

'Are you okay with this, Mimi?' he said abruptly. 'About coming back with me to the house? I mean, I threw it at you at the last minute.' He grimaced. 'And it's not as if I've been considerate of your wishes so far.'

Her stomach somersaulted. 'Are you *not* okay?' she asked. Was he trying to be fair? To atone for his behaviour? Or had he changed his mind?

'Yes. I mean, no.' He frowned. 'Or do I mean yes? Whatever.'

She felt his fingers tighten around hers and, lifting her hand to his mouth, he kissed it gently.

'I really do want you to come and stay with me, but I want to make sure that's what you want too.'

'It is.' She bit into her smile. 'It really, *really* is.'

Whatever was in her heart would wait. It would have to wait. Right now what mattered was the heat in his eyes…a heat that felt like a caress against her skin.

Heart hammering, she leaned forward and kissed him. It was a long, slow, deepening kiss, and hunger was zig-zagging through her body as he slid his hand around her waist. She arched against him restlessly, her fingers sliding through his hair.

'Mimi...' He groaned her name and then pulled his mouth from hers, breathing out unsteadily. 'We need to stop now.'

'Why?' she whispered against his mouth. 'Or is that your way of saying you won't be held responsible for what happens next?'

His glittering gaze locked with hers. 'Right now I'd say I'm definitely suffering from diminished responsibility.'

'Really?' She pressed her hand against his trousers. 'It doesn't feel very diminished to me.'

His eyes were trained on hers. 'We'll be home in five minutes.'

From somewhere inside his jacket his phone began to buzz, and after kissing him lightly on the mouth she slipped free of his arms. 'Don't worry,' she said softly. 'I can wait.'

Gritting his teeth, he yanked the phone from his pocket. 'This had better be important, Rebecca.'

The car slowed, then stopped, and with her head still spinning from Basa's kiss Mimi opened the door.

As she stepped out onto the pavement a group

of maybe thirty *paparazzi* surged forward, seemingly from nowhere, pinning her against the car. She blinked, blinded briefly by the camera flashes, her hand fumbling for something to grab on to as they called her name.

'*Mimi, over here!*'

One of the men pushed his microphone into her face, his nostrils flaring with excitement.

'*Mimi, what's happening with you and Basa? Are you two an item?*'

She turned away, trying to cover her face with her hand. But, sensing her paralysis, they were hemming her in, all of them pushing closer, so close she could smell their collective aftershave.

'*How long's it been going on? Are you living together, Mimi?*'

'*What do you think those pensioners will say when they find out about your affair?*'

Her head was reeling, her skin crawling with panic, and she was finding it hard to breathe, much less move.

'What the—?'

She heard Basa swear violently under his breath, and then he was beside her, shielding her with his body, his size and the unforgiving expression on his face creating a space around them. He pulled her against him as he and his driver shoved their way through the clamouring pack and up the stairs into his house.

Her legs felt as though they were made of feathers. 'It's okay… I'm okay,' she mumbled.

'Of course you're not okay.' Basa's voice was taut, like a sail snapping in high wind. 'Here, sit down.'

They were in a living room, and gratefully Mimi sat down on a dark green velvet sofa as their driver followed them into the room.

'I'm so sorry, Mr Caine.'

'It's fine, Paul. Just get the car parked and then get someone to drop off another one. Nothing too eye-catching.'

Mimi was shivering. Her teeth were chattering and she felt sick. It had all happened so fast. One minute she had been in the car, kissing Basa, and the next it had been as if time had gone into reverse, and she was back outside the home she had once shared with her mum and Charlie.

Basa was holding out a glass of tawny liquid. 'Drink this.'

It was brandy. She didn't like brandy. But she

drank it anyway, and after a moment breathed out unsteadily.

'I don't understand,' she said slowly. 'How did they know we would be here?'

Basa's face was like stone, and there was a roughness to his voice when he spoke.

'Somebody saw us in that street in Buenos Aires. They took photos of us. I guess from a distance it must have looked like a lovers' tiff.'

He held up his phone and she stared at the screen, wondering how something so small could cause so much damage. Her heart quivered. It felt strange, looking at herself and Basa together. The photo was nearly a week old, and in that week they had gone from enemies to lovers. But the camera didn't lie, and even though they were clearly arguing, she could almost see the pulse of attraction between them, in the angle of their bodies and the tilt of her heads.

And someone else had noticed it too.

She felt a flare of panic and her hands balled into fists, but Basa didn't notice. He was staring past her into the distance, as though he was watching something unfold that was visible only to him.

'My PA got a call ten minutes ago, asking her to confirm that you and I are a couple. That was her on the phone. She was trying to warn me, but she was too late.'

'I'm sorry,' she whispered.

She saw that his muscles were straining against his suit jacket, but even if they hadn't been she could feel his frustration, his anger vibrating off his skin like radio waves. And she couldn't blame him for being angry. He had warned her back in Buenos Aires about this happening and she had ignored him. And now they were all going to pay for her recklessness in leaving his home.

All of them—including Alicia.

Her best friend. Who was getting married in just a few months' time.

Her heart stopped beating.

She felt a sharp stab of realisation as the air in her lungs seemed to thin. How was this going to affect the wedding? And how must Alicia be feeling now she had heard about Mimi and Basa allegedly having some kind of relationship? Of course she wanted to believe that Alicia would be happy, but even if she was the timing was so bad. Mimi felt as though the room was tilting, as though she was drunk, but it wasn't the brandy making the world spin off its axis. It was *her*. She'd messed everything up.

His next words—or rather the distance in his voice as he spoke them—confirmed her fears.

'It's my fault. I should have made it clearer to you what was at stake if you left the house.'

But she had known what was at stake.

Her lungs seemed to shrivel, along with any hopes she might have had of making things work with Basa. Those hopes were gone now, thrown away by her in that smoke-filled street in Buenos Aires.

'You did tell me,' she said quietly. 'I just didn't believe you.'

It was a fitting conclusion to a relationship that had been destined not to happen. How could it when neither one of them had ever known when the other was telling the truth.

'This isn't about what I told you or what you believed. This is about you and me sleeping together—and that's on me as much as it is on you. More so,' he added. 'I'm in the public eye twenty-four-seven, so I knew the risks. I ignored them because you were worth it. So don't blame yourself.'

There was a beat of silence, and she felt a slow trickle of despair work its way down her spine as he pulled out his phone. He was being so reasonable, so nice, but whatever he said she knew he was just being kind out of guilt or concern.

She watched miserably as his expression hardened at the sight of something on his screen.

'What matters now is damage limitation,' he said. 'But you don't need to worry. I'm going to take care of this.'

Mimi stared at him, her heartbeat slowing. He was a good man. A good brother. A good son. He would work day and night to protect his family, to protect her, and she loved him for that. But she wasn't his responsibility and she didn't want to *be* his responsibility. Nor was she going to throw her best friend under a bus for the sake of a few passion-filled days in Patagonia.

So there were two ways of doing this.

She could sit it out and wait for Basa to grow tired of her—because he *would* grow tired of her. And he might even end up hating her again once the media got stuck in. Or she could make it easy for both of them. Make it so that her best friend's wedding wasn't overshadowed by the scandal that had so nearly ruined the Caine family two years ago.

'Would it be okay if I used your bathroom?' Her hair had come loose as they'd pushed their way into the house, and she touched it now by way of explanation.

'Of course. You aren't hurt, are you?'

His eyes widened suddenly, his pupils merging with his irises, and she felt as if she was falling into two dark pools, her body weighted with rocks.

She shook her head. She wasn't hurt. Not in the way he meant.

He showed her to the bathroom, and after closing the door she sat down on the side of the bath. It was all over before it had even begun. Just like every other part of her life, she had ruined it. Driving her father away, wrecking her career, and now sabotaging her relationship with the only man she had ever wanted.

Last time *he* had walked away. Now it was her turn. She didn't want to do it, but she couldn't blight the lives of the two people she loved most in the world. Nor could she bear this flame between her and Basa to be slowly extinguished by the mistakes of the past.

She reached into her bag and pulled out her phone.

When she came back into the living room, Basa was on his own phone.

'Look, I have to go, but I'll call you back later,' he said to the caller, then paused, his dark gaze resting on Mimi's face. 'Yeah, I'll tell her.'

He hung up and tossed his phone onto the sofa. 'That was Alicia.'

'I know.' There had been a softness in his voice, a protectiveness she'd recognised and loved, that had told her he was speaking to someone he loved. And this was her chance to protect him.

'Is she okay? Is your dad okay?'

His face tensed, and although she hadn't moved she could almost feel the space between them widen.

'They will be. They're holed up at Alicia's flat, but Philip's there, and my security team is going to move them once it gets dark.'

She winced inwardly. He must be so worried about Alicia, and even more so about his father, and yet he was playing it down. The matter-of-fact way he was talking about his life imploding made everything a thousand times worse.

'You're a good man.' Mimi tried to smile, but who could smile when their heart was breaking?

Basa frowned, and she knew that something of what she was feeling must show in her face.

'What is it?' he asked.

She took a deep breath, forcing herself to speak past the lump in her throat. 'I can't stay here—not now. Not with—'

He cut her off. 'This isn't how it's going be for ever.'

'Maybe not,' she said quietly. 'But we don't have for ever, Basa. Alicia is getting married in less than three months. And that's what's important here, isn't it? Making sure her wedding isn't ruined by a lot of messy headlines.'

She waited, the lump in her throat swelling. Part of her—the wretched, hopelessly in love with him part—was hoping that he would pull her against him like he had on the jet, and then in the car, and tell her that he loved her, that she was what was important to him, now and for ever. But of course she knew he wouldn't say that.

So before he had a chance to reply she said quickly, 'If Paul could give me a lift I have somewhere I can stay.'

It was his opportunity to stop her, and there was a part of her heart that trembled with the hope that he would. But he didn't say anything, and she felt something split apart inside her as he nodded slowly.

Five minutes later Basa led her through the house and out through the garden.

'You won't have any trouble leaving this way.' He glanced at the modest, nondescript saloon idling by the kerb. 'Especially not in this car. Just tell Paul where you want to go.'

His smile was taut, the muscles in his jaw tense like piano wire.

'Thank you.' It hurt her to smile—more so to look at his face.

'Mimi.'

Her heart leapt against her ribs as he pulled her into his arms.

'It'll be fine. I promise.'

She inhaled his scent, wishing she could hold it inside of her for ever, so that she would always have a part of him, but as his grip loosened she let go of her breath.

In the car, she tried to stare straight ahead, but as Paul started the engine she couldn't stop herself from turning back to look at Basa. For a few half-seconds his dark eyes rested on her face, and then the car was moving, and she sat there, her stomach clenched with hope, waiting for him to come after her, willing him to yank open the door and tell her that he loved her.

But as the car turned into the road and they joined the mid-morning traffic she realised that, far from wanting her to stay, he had been willing her to leave.

Three hours later she was curled up on the sofa in her friend Emma's tiny flat, the curtains drawn, a mug of undrunk tea on the table in front of her. Normally she loved a cup of tea, but this one had grown cold as she'd stared blankly at the book in her lap.

She had showered and changed out of what she'd been wearing, hoping the hot water and clean clothes would help shift the lethargy that had overtaken her as Paul drove her to Emma's address. But it hadn't helped. Sitting here alone, with damp hair and an oversized sweater, made it all feel much more real and final.

Glancing over at her phone, she resisted the urge to pick it up and check for messages or missed calls. She had left a message for Alicia, apologising, and then called her mum, who hadn't picked up, so she'd left a message for her too. From Basa there had been nothing.

Her throat tightened, and she felt the heat of tears. But why would there be?

He was probably under siege from reporters and lawyers, and even if he wasn't, why would he want to talk to *her*? He might have said he didn't blame her, but that would change over time. And then there was Alicia...

Her stomach clenched. There would be no wedding film now. In fact, she wasn't going to go to the wedding at all. She felt her breathing slow, for she knew how upset Lissy would be. It might even be the end of their friendship.

The dread in her stomach was hot and stinging, and slippery like a jellyfish. Not to go would be cruel, but to go would be worse in the long run, for it would be wilfully negligent of the consequences. It had to be this way. Like amputating a limb with frostbite. You had to lose the leg to save the life, and Lissy and Philip were worth saving a hundred times over.

Basa too.

His whole life had been spent looking after other people—looking after his father, parenting his sister, taking over the family business. Not only to protect his family, but also to protect the livelihoods of all those people who worked for him. And he wasn't even thirty. He'd already sacrificed so much. She wasn't going to make him sacrifice anything else.

Someone was ringing the doorbell.

Her whole body tensed.

The bones in her legs had locked tight and for a moment she couldn't move. It couldn't be a reporter—they didn't bother waiting for you to answer. They lifted open the letterbox and shouted their questions through the door.

Her heart slid sideways. Only three people knew she was here. Emma, Paul and Basa.

Sliding the chain of the latch, she opened the door with a rush of anticipation.

But it wasn't Basa.

It was her mother.

'I got your message. I'm sorry I didn't get here sooner. I went away for a couple of days with a friend and the signal was terrible.'

Mimi swallowed. 'You didn't have to come back, Mum.'

Her mother frowned. 'Of course I came back—you're my daughter. I'm not going to leave you to fight off those wolves on your own.'

Stepping into the flat, she closed the door and pulled Mimi into a hug. For a moment Mimi stiffened, trying to pull away, but her mum wouldn't let her and finally she gave in to what she had been wanting to do since leaving Basa's house. She burst into tears.

'It will be all right.' Leaning forward, her mother smoothed Mimi's hair away from her face. 'It's just a photo, not a court case.'

'A photo of me and Basa. And people hold grudges, Mum. They hold on to things—to feelings—for years.'

'I know,' her mum said quietly. 'I held on to my past for far too long. But you've just spent a week with Basa—alone on an island. Everybody should let go of the past, and if you two can then so can everyone else.'

Mimi blew her nose. She'd expected her mum to be crying, or at least panicking, but she was calm—relaxed, even.

'I don't think Basa will ever really let go of it. Not if he wants to protect his family.'

'Did he say that?'

'No, not in so many words,' Mimi said slowly. 'But he didn't try to stop me leaving.'

'Maybe letting you go was his way of trying to protect you?'

She stared at her mother helplessly. 'I can't think like that, Mum. I just want it to be over. I don't want to feel like this any more. I don't want to feel anything. That's why I walked away.'

Her mother leaned over and wiped a tear from Mimi's cheek. 'But you can't walk away from love, Mimi. And you *do* love him, don't you?'

Hearing her mum say it out loud broke her open.

'But I messed it up—like I always mess everything up.' Tears were streaming down her face now, too many to wipe away.

Her mum frowned. 'Such as what?'

'Like you and Dad. You were so much in love, and then I came along and ruined it. And then I pushed you into marrying Charlie so you wouldn't be on your own.'

More tears escaped and she brushed them away with her sleeve.

'Is that what I made you think?'

Glancing up into her mother's face, Mimi saw that she looked shocked and horrified.

'Mimi, that's not what happened. I know I used to talk a lot about how much me and your dad were in love, but that was only because I wanted to give you something positive about our relationship. I wanted you to know that you came out of real passion. It wasn't your fault your dad left me. We just weren't right together.'

She frowned.

'And as for Charlie—you didn't push me into anything. I was a grown woman and I liked Charlie. I didn't love him, but I wanted you to have a dad, and nice things, so I ignored all his little lies. If anyone messed up, it was me.'

Mimi shook her head, her hands balling into fists. 'But I've made a mess of my film too, and it was my fault that the photo was taken in Buenos Aires. Everything I touch, I ruin.'

'That's not true. You put yourself out there and sometimes things go wrong. But I am so proud of you. You are brave and talented and loyal, and any man—including Bautista Caine—would be lucky to have you.'

Her mother was crying now too.

'And, frankly, I will tell him so myself.'

She reached for Mimi's phone.

'No, Mum.' Mimi tried to grab it. 'It's too late.'

Shaking her head, her mum smiled weakly. 'Love doesn't come with a deadline, or hide away in the shadows.' She handed Mimi the phone. 'And neither should you, darling.'

CHAPTER TEN

PICKING UP THE top newspaper from the pile beside him, Basa scanned the front page before expertly flipping through the rest of the paper. His PA had been sending the papers over each morning since the story broke, ringing any relevant sections with a marker pen, but his dark gaze found nothing to interest him today.

The tabloids had a couple of stories each—nothing new, just the Buenos Aires photo padded out with some additional paragraphs about the trial.

He let out a breath and scooped the papers onto the floor. Overall, was not too bad. Probably tomorrow, the day after at the latest, the genie would be back in the lamp and by the time Alicia exchanged her vows with Philip the whole episode would be nothing but a footnote.

The worst was over. He had moved fast and effectively and, having been through it once before—twice if you included his mother's accident—he had known what needed to be done to kill the story. He'd done it, and now his sister's wedding would no longer have the spectre of scandal hanging over it.

Everything was under control. He should be happy. He was, of course. And yet his happiness felt staged, as if he was an actor playing himself. None of it felt real. And he wasn't sure it ever would...without Mimi.

He stared down at his phone. Alicia had called and left several messages, saying it was nothing urgent, to call her back, but from Mimi there had been nothing.

Unsurprisingly.

His paralysed silence when she had announced she was leaving had not exactly given her any incentive to stay in touch, and now it was nearly a week since she had got into that car with Paul.

Watching her leave, he'd wanted to chase after her, to ask her to stay. But he hadn't been able to ask or expect her to do that—not knowing what he did.

Two years ago she and her mother had been chased, snapped and vilified just for the crime of being related to Charlie and Raymond. It hadn't mattered to anyone, himself included, that they were innocent, unknowing bystanders. They had been judged fair game and treated accordingly.

His shoulders tensed and he felt his heart contracting with rage and regret. Mimi and her mother had had nobody to protect them—no security team to hold back the photographers, no lawyers fighting to defend their reputation, their name. They had been helpless and scared. And after watching her face as the *paparazzi* had penned her against his car the other day, he knew that fear hadn't dissipated over time.

And that was why he hadn't stopped her from leaving.

He hadn't been able to ask her to stay for him—not after everything else he had demanded she do. He hadn't been able to make her go through all that again, so he had let her go.

But he missed her.

From the moment he woke up in the morning and all through his restless nights she was there. No matter what he was doing she was in his head. He could hear her voice, her laughter, and sometimes when he closed his eyes he could feel her hair sliding over his skin, the soft whisper of her breath against his mouth.

He stood up, loneliness lapping like waves against his heart, and made his way to the window, as if by moving he could shift the feeling of fullness in his chest. Running a hand over his face, he stared at his reflection. He hadn't shaved for the last three days, and instead of his usual suit and tie he was wearing joggers and a T-shirt. It was slack of him, but the effort of dressing seemed to be beyond him right now.

As did eating.

Unless whisky counted as a food.

He glanced over at the half-empty decanter. He wasn't a big drinker, but he needed something in the evenings to blot out the ache, something to fill the hollowed-out space inside his chest.

He heard the sound of approaching footsteps. He took a breath and composed his face before he turned, fully expecting to see his housekeeper, Annie, her mouth set in a conciliatory smile as she offered the tray of food she would be carrying, for it wouldn't have escaped her notice that he had skipped breakfast again.

But it wasn't Annie. It was his sister Alicia and she didn't look the least bit conciliatory.

'I've been calling you all morning,' she said accusingly. 'Why didn't you pick up?'

'Sorry, I was just going to call back. I got caught up in something,' he lied. Crossing the room, he pulled her into a hug. 'We can talk now…catch up properly. Would you like a drink?'

Her eyes darted to the decanter. 'It's a bit early for whisky.'

He released her. 'I meant tea or coffee.'

Her face softened. 'Coffee, please. And a talk would be lovely.'

'So, what do you want me for?' he asked.

They were sitting on the sofa and, glancing over at his sister, he thought how well she looked. Her dark hair was shining and her skin looked almost luminous.

Being in love suited her, and it also seemed to be acting as a protective shield, so that although initially she had been upset by the news story she had quickly recovered her equilibrium. Equally surprisingly, his father had too. In fact, out of the three of them, he was the one who was struggling to deal with it. Not the practicalities, of course, but emotionally.

'I wanted to invite you to lunch.'

He stared at her blankly. Lunch? The thought made his stomach clench like a fist. He knew it was selfish, but the last thing he felt like doing was sitting down with Alicia and Philip and watching them gaze into each other's eyes.

'I'm not sure, Lissy...' He glanced down at the pile of papers on the floor, seeking and finding an excuse. 'I need to be here in case something kicks off.'

'What could possibly kick off?' Alicia frowned. 'You haven't left the house in days and Mimi's gone AWOL. All the photographers have cleared off.'

His chest tightened. It was the first time in a week that he'd heard anyone say Mimi's name out loud, and it felt like a kick to the stomach.

'Basa?'

His sister tilted her head and he realised she was still waiting for a reply.

He hesitated a moment longer, and then, flexing his hands, he said. 'Have you talked to her?'

There was a pause. 'We've texted,' she said after a moment. 'She's with her mum. They're doing okay.' Alicia hesitated. 'She was worried about all of us—about everything being dragged up again—but I told her it was fine.'

Basa nodded. It seemed crazy that only a couple of weeks ago he'd been desperate to break up their friendship. Crazy that he'd thought he could. Or should.

Alicia cleared her throat. 'I told her that she and I would be fine whatever happened—even if what the papers are saying is true.'

He stared at her, the ramifications of her words bumping off the walls as she put down her coffee cup.

'Why are you asking me? Why don't you just talk to her yourself?'

Something was loosening inside him. He could feel it slipping sideways, but it was just out of reach, so he turned his attention back to his sister.

'That's not a good idea.'

Alicia's soft brown eyes narrowed. 'I don't see why,' she protested. 'You wouldn't be asking me if I'd talked to her if you didn't care.'

'I care about you and Dad,' he said. 'You are my priority.'

'Well, maybe it's time we weren't!'

His head jerked up at the frustration in her voice.

'Look, I love you. You're the best brother anyone could have and you've always been there for me—and I know Daddy feels the same. I know—' He tried to interrupt but she held up her hand to silence him 'I know he feels the same because I've talked to him about it. We are fine and you need to stop putting your life on hold for us.'

'I'm not doing that, Lissy.'

'Yes, you are. You're using the past as a shield, so you don't have to face your feelings.'

'That's not what I'm doing.'

He tried to keep his voice even, but it was hard with her staring at him with that disbelieving expression on her face. For a moment neither of them spoke, and then she sighed.

'So why don't you call her?'

He felt his muscles tighten beneath his skin.

It was the same question he'd been asking himself for days. Asking, but never answering.

'You know why.'

Meeting his gaze, she cleared her throat. 'I do. I'm just wondering when you're going to stop pretending you don't.'

The air was hot and thin in his lungs, and he made himself take a breath. 'I'm not pretending anything.'

Her eyes filled with tears, and suddenly her lip was trembling.

'Yes, you *are*. You're pretending that this news story still needs you to manage it. You're pretending that I'm still fifteen and Daddy's still ill. But mostly you're pretending you don't love Mimi when you so obviously do.'

His shoulders tensed. Her words were scraping at the graze around his heart and he was conscious of his breath filling his chest. His heart shifted, growing lighter, as if something heavy had been lifted from it.

Of course he loved her!

That was why he'd been so devastated by her behaviour that night at Fairbourne and why he'd insisted she come to Argentina and Patagonia.

Why watching her drive off in that car and go out of his life had made him feel undone.

'I don't… I don't—'

For a moment the power of speech abandoned him. He couldn't finish the sentence. And he couldn't lie to his sister or to himself any more.

But he couldn't tell the truth either.

Back on the island Mimi had said that Alicia thought love was the solution to everything, and she was right. His sister was a fully paid-up believer in the power of love. How was he supposed to explain to her that on this occasion love wasn't enough?

By nature Alicia had always been sweetly optimistic, and her optimism often tipped over into naivety. It was what he loved about her, and why he'd been so protective of her all his life. But no matter how right she was now, how much he wanted to follow his heart, he knew that the world wasn't ready for a relationship between Bautista Caine and Mimi Miller. He only had to look at the aftershocks of one blurred photo to know that.

Going public with their relationship would magnify those problems tenfold, and he couldn't do that to Mimi. He'd seen how shaken she was by those few minutes with the *paparazzi*, knew how terrified she was of the past being resurrected—for hadn't she told him that was why she had given up the fight to get her embargoed film released? She had learnt the hard way that not all publicity was good publicity.

Alicia pulled him into a hug. He could feel

her heart beating and the dampness of her cheek against his.

'I'm not going to try and change your mind,' she said. 'I just want you to remember that you have a life of your own to live.'

She released him. 'Look, I have to go, but promise me you'll come to lunch? About one.' Her brown eyes flickered over his joggers. 'And get dressed. Otherwise I'll be forced to put on my unicorn onesie.'

Nodding, he managed to smile. He could see she wouldn't take no for an answer, and what else was he going to do today?

His heart felt suddenly heavy against his ribs. Without Mimi, what was he going to do with the rest of his life?

Two hours later he let himself into Alicia's flat, holding a bottle of wine. He had showered, and changed into khakis and a polo shirt, but left the stubble. Right now his face felt a little treacherous, and having it there was somehow reassuring—like having a mask.

He liked Alicia's flat. In a word, it was charming. Big enough to feel comfortable, but small enough to feel cosy, and decorated with an easy elegance that she'd inherited from his mother. Today, though, it felt oddly quiet.

'You didn't say what we were having,' he called out, walking into the kitchen, 'but I went with white.'

'White sounds lovely.'

He froze, his whole body pushing back against his thousand and one involuntary reactions to that familiar, soft voice while his gaze was pulled to where Mimi was standing in the doorway, wearing faded jeans and a soft blue jumper, her long blonde hair loose over her shoulders, her eyes fixed on his face.

There was a good two minutes of silence. Mimi could feel her heart in her throat. She could hardly believe it was only a week since she had last seen him. It felt as if a whole decade had passed. And after the wild grandeur of Patagonia being with him here in Alicia's homely kitchen felt almost surreal.

He stood up, his chair scraping against the wooden floor. 'You two set this up.'

It wasn't a question, but she nodded. 'I'm not really equipped for roadside abductions.'

She tried to smile, but her lips wouldn't co-operate. Her whole body felt stiff and unwieldy. She was nervous, but she was also having to push back against the urge to cross the room and kiss him. It hurt to be so close and not be able to touch him, like having to hold her breath too long underwater.

'Mimi—'

'Basa—'

They both spoke at once.

He stared at her for a moment, and then he cleared his throat. 'After you.'

It was her chance to talk, to say what she needed to say, only now she was here she was paralysed, mute with fear that she would say the wrong thing.

But even she couldn't mess up three little words.

'I love you.'

She took a step forward, her limbs loosening as she spoke.

'I should have said it before, but I was scared. And I know you probably don't feel the same way, and I know the world doesn't want us to be together—'

'It doesn't matter what the world wants.'

Her heart jolted against her ribs as he began walking towards her, his dark eyes locked on hers.

'It's what *we* want—you and me. And I don't want— I don't—' Breaking off, he breathed out unsteadily. 'I don't ever want to be apart from you again.'

She couldn't breathe. Tears were filling her eyes and she could see that his face was pale and taut with the effort of holding back tears of his own.

'Why did you leave?'

He spoke shakily and she knew that it mattered. She knew that the shake in his voice meant he cared, and that gave her strength.

'I was scared. It was my fault they had that photo and I thought I'd messed up again.'

His hands caught her shoulders.

'It was just a mistake, Mimi. I get papped all the time—even when I'm on my own,' he said fiercely.

'I know, and I can see that now, but all my life things have gone wrong—my dad leaving, Charlie and Raymond stealing from all those poor pensioners, my film getting embargoed, you and me that night…'

'None of that was your fault.'

'I want to believe that, but it's hard to trust yourself when nobody else trusts you.'

'*I* trust you.'

His hands tightened against her shoulders and she felt as if her heart was going to burst as he pulled her into his arms, holding her tightly against him so she could feel his heartbeat merge with hers.

'And I need you.'

He pulled her closer, burying his face in her hair.

'I've been so miserable without you.'

'Why?' Her voice faltered. 'Why were you miserable, Basa?'

His eyes were dark and soft and unguarded. 'Because I love you.'

He leaned in and kissed her, his hands sliding up to capture her face as her heart slipped its moorings.

'I think I might even have loved you before we met.' He frowned. 'You know that night at Fairbourne…it felt so right—as though we'd been fighting our way to one another across time and space. The other day when you left I should have stopped you, but I was scared. For so long I've focused on other people's lives and not on my own. I've used the past as a reason not to think about my present, and when you said you couldn't stay…that was the first time in my life I've had to think about what *I* really wanted. And I panicked.'

He kissed the tears from her face.

'But I'm not panicking now.'

Mimi swallowed. 'And what *do* you want?'

'I want you,' he said softly. 'Because I love you. Totally and immeasurably.'

Reaching up, she stroked his face. 'And I love you.'

He stared at her in silence, his beautiful face showing everything he was feeling, and then he lowered his mouth and kissed her again, hungrily, kissed her until the past was forgotten and all that mattered was the two of them.

From inside her jeans pocket her phone vibrated twice. Loosening her grip, Mimi looked up into Basa's eyes, a blush creeping across her cheeks.

'That'll be Alicia. I made her promise to text in case it all went wrong.' She pulled out her phone. 'I'll have to text her back or she'll think the worst.'

She frowned.

'What is it?' Basa looked down at her.

'I don't understand,' Mimi said slowly. 'It's my lawyer. Apparently my film has been released for distribution.'

'Is that right?'

The teasing note in his voice made her look up from her phone. 'Did you have something to do with this?'

His dark eyes rested on her face. 'I might have applied a little pressure in the right places.' He pulled her closer, his gaze drifting slowly over her stunned face. 'I wanted to surprise you when we got back to England, but it's a little late now.'

Her pulse accelerated as he smiled slowly.

'So maybe it could be an early engagement present instead.'

She drew in a deep breath, trying to absorb his words. 'Are you asking me to marry you?'

He nodded, his face so serious and sweet she wanted to cry.

'I am—if you'll have me.'

She was both laughing and crying now.

'Hang on—is that a yes? Only, I don't want

there to be any more misunderstandings between us,' he said softly.

'There's no misunderstanding.' Blinking back
tears of happiness, she lifted her face to his and
kissed him. It's definitely a yes.'

EPILOGUE

GLANCING UP AT the towering cobalt-blue sky, Mimi breathed in the smell of the sage that had been disturbed by the wheels of the SUV and instantly felt all tension leave her body.

For the last few days she and Basa had been staying with Alicia and Philip at the *palacio* in Buenos Aires, but yesterday they had travelled across the country to Patagonia. And it felt incredible to be here again in this beautiful epic landscape.

Basa and Philip had gone straight to the island, but she and Alicia had spent the night at the newly opened Guanaco eco-lodge, for some last-minute pampering before joining them.

And now they were stepping off the jetty into the boat.

It would be her third visit to the island, but her reverence and sense of wonder at its beauty and solitude was still the same and, taking a calming breath, she gazed across the unbroken surface of the lake, a pulse of happiness beating down her spine.

The ducks and swans were squabbling in the shallows, but their splashing and the rhythmic slap of the water against the shore were the only sounds to break the silence. Up above her the sun was almost white, but the lightest of breezes took the edge of the midday heat so that it felt exactly like the perfect spring day.

And it was, she thought, her heart beginning to beat a little faster. It was perfect—and in so many ways other than the weather.

'Penny for them? Or are they priceless?'

She'd been so deep in thought that Alicia's voice seemed to come out of nowhere and, turning, she found her friend smiling at her. It had been a pattern over the last few days and, meeting Alicia's gentle gaze, she grimaced apologetically. 'Sorry.'

Taking her hand, Alicia shook her head. 'Don't be. I think it's lovely.' Her face softened. 'Basa's just the same.' She giggled. 'Philip told me, but don't tell Basa I told you.'

Mimi laughed. 'I won't.' She gave her friend's hand a squeeze. 'I haven't been too bad, have I?'

'No, of course not.' Alicia frowned. 'Obviously you were nervous about making your engagement public, but we all were a little bit.'

She *had* been nervous. Actually, make that terrified. But, despite her fears that people would condemn her or, worse, condemn Basa, both the media and the public had seen their engagement as a positive footnote to the pension scandal—a kind of 'love conquers all' story.

'There's your mum,' Alicia said quietly.

Mimi felt her eyes start to burn. Her mum had been so fantastic these last six months. She could see that over time her mother had been slowly emerging from the hibernation of despair and regret, and seeing her daughter so happy seemed to have given her the final nudge she needed to take back control of her life.

Now, not only did she have a new hobby—wild swimming—but a new haircut and a new man.

'Hi, Mum,' she said warmly as they disembarked.

'Oh, darling.' Her mother's eyes were bright with tears, and her smile was trembling as they hugged.

They linked arms and, with Alicia following, they walked along the jetty across to the house, where four men were standing in a semi-circle, waiting for them.

Philip. Robert. Basa. And Emiliano, the celebrant who was going to conduct their wedding ceremony.

Something was dislodged inside her as her gaze rested on the man who was already her husband.

They had married at the Civil Registry Office in Buenos Aires, with only Alicia and Philip for witnesses. Neither of them had wanted a fuss, but both of them had known that they wanted to repeat the ceremony out in Patagonia, on the island where their love had finally overcome the scandal of their past.

And they were no longer alone in putting the past behind them. Both Robert Caine and her mother had accepted their relationship—accepted and encouraged it. She glanced affectionately back at her friend. For Alicia, of course, the past had never been an obstacle.

Her mother gave her arm a squeeze, and as they stopped in front of Basa her heart began to pound. He looked so incredibly handsome in a dark suit and pale blue shirt and, in a gesture towards the new openness they shared, the top button of his shirt was undone.

'Hi,' he said softly.

Gazing into his eyes, she saw tears that mirrored her own and felt her chest swell with absolute unconditional love as he took her hand in his.

The ceremony seemed to pass in seconds. But then from the moment Mimi had stepped off the boat, her veil fluttering in the breeze, time had ceased to matter, Basa thought, his chest tightening as she looked up into his eyes.

Her pale blonde hair was caught loosely at the nape of her neck and she was wearing a simple blue *ombré* slip dress the same colour as the sapphire engagement ring he had given her, for the mix of gold and blue reminded him of the sky that day they had spent in the hot air balloon.

He didn't think he had ever seen her look more beautiful.

Speaking his vows, watching Mimi speak hers, he felt his heart would burst—and not just with love, but with the knowledge of how close they had come to losing each other.

They hadn't been apart at all since that day in Alicia's kitchen, and last night he'd missed her unbearably. Now, despite the emotional intensity of the words they were saying to one another, he almost wished the ceremony was over, so he could pull her into his arms and hold her close.

Of course she was already his wife, but the ceremony in Buenos Aires had felt like a simple legal formality. He glanced past her at the clusters of evergreens, at the high cloud-capped peaks in the distance. For him, *this* was what their marriage was about. Standing here with the epic majesty of nature as their witness, with everyone they loved beside them.

But not quite everyone, he thought sadly. Although he could sense his mother in Alicia's soft eyes and gentle smile.

After the ceremony was over they ate a late lunch—lamb, straight from the hot yellow blaze of Lionel's willow-framed *asado*. Then there were speeches, and everyone toasted the marriage with a Merlot from Robert's estate. Seeing both their families talking and smiling in the sunshine made their marriage feel doubly blessed.

Much, much later, when the fire was a dull orange core, everyone retreated inside the house. But Basa led Mimi down to where Claudia had lit the deck with hundreds of tiny night lights.

Pulling her down onto the lounger beside him, he kissed her softly. 'I missed you yesterday.'

'I missed you too,' she whispered. 'But it was worth it. For today.'

He buried his face in her hair, breathing in her scent. 'Are you sure? I mean, I know we decided not to go for a big wedding…'

His sister's wedding had been vast. A three-day affair, with hundreds of guests, starting with a tango-themed party at the house in Buenos Aires and ending with the ceremony here in Patagonia. It had been the perfect society event, but he'd spent the whole time feeling grateful that he wasn't going to have to go through all that with his own wedding. Now he wanted to be certain that Mimi felt the same way too.

Her blue eyes flickered in the candlelight. 'I'm sure. I mean, look at this…' She waved up at the star-pierced darkening sky. 'We have our very own cathedral, all to ourselves—and, besides, I have everything and everyone that matters right here.'

Her cheeks were flushed with happiness, her eyes alive with warmth and love.

He tilted her face up to his and said softly, 'I do too. Now and for ever.'

And, lowering his mouth, he kissed her until their heads were filled with stars that were brighter than the ones in the sky above…

* * * * *

LET'S TALK

Romance

For exclusive extracts, competitions
and special offers, find us online:

f facebook.com/millsandboon

[instagram] @millsandboonuk

[twitter] @millsandboon

Or get in touch on 0844 844 1351*

For all the latest titles coming soon,
visit millsandboon.co.uk/nextmonth

*Calls cost 7p per minute plus your phone company's price per
minute access charge

Want even more
ROMANCE?

Join our bookclub today!

'Mills & Boon books, the perfect way to escape for an hour or so.'

Miss W. Dyer

'Excellent service, promptly delivered and very good subscription choices.'

Miss A. Pearson

'You get fantastic special offers and the chance to get books before they hit the shops'

Mrs V. Hall

Visit millsandbook.co.uk/Bookclub and save on brand new books.

MILLS & BOON